SECRETS OF
ECHO MOON

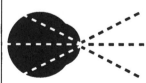

This Large Print Book carries the
Seal of Approval of N.A.V.H.

SECRETS OF ECHO MOON

Jill Giencke

Thorndike Press • Thorndike, Maine

KBOM LE WB GP IC FK BH MH AS

Published in 1997 by arrangement with Jill Giencke.

Thorndike Large Print ® Candlelight Series.

The tree indicium is a trademark of Thorndike Press.

The text of this Large Print edition is unabridged.
Other aspects of the book may vary from the original edition.

Set in 16 pt. Plantin by Rick Gundberg.

Printed in the United States on permanent paper.

Library of Congress Cataloging in Publication Data

Giencke, Jill, 1959–
     Secrets of Echo Moon / Jill Giencke.
        p.   cm.
     ISBN 0-7862-1188-1 (lg. print : hc : alk. paper)
     1. Large type books.   I. Title.
[PS3557.I258S43   1997]
     813′.54—dc21   97-21452

To my family for all their encouragement.
To Neal for all his love.

Chapter One

What have you gotten yourself into? I thought, leaning against the decidedly filthy railing of the old boat. Beneath my feet, the deck shook and shuddered as the engine rumbled us along.

Disappearing rapidly from sight, back on dry ground, was my car — and my old life. Not for the first time I had to shake my head and blink. It was crazy!

One day I'd been minding my own business — literally, it's a bookstore called the Old Curiosity Shop — and the next I was on a boat headed for a place called Echo Moon Island, located about five miles off the coast of Wisconsin in Lake Michigan. I'd never been this far north before, except once as a child when my parents and I had taken the long ride along Highway 2 to visit some relatives in Michigan. I wasn't sure I wanted to be here now, but the opportunity seemed too good to pass up.

A man named Andrew Clayton had written to me about a month earlier. He said he'd gotten my name from the local university's library-science department, where I had gotten my degree in library science last year. They'd recommended me as a person who knew a lot about rare books, who specialized in them, actually. Well, that was certainly true. I'd spent my childhood living above the bookstore my parents owned, surrounded by books on every side. Mom wasn't much for housekeeping. "Too many important things to do," she always said. So the dishes weren't always done, but the books were treated with tender, loving care.

Our "library" was the extra bedroom, and we spent many happy hours there, the three of us, each reading our favorite author on quiet Saturday nights.

Of course, after the accident I found myself sole owner of the Old Curiosity Shop, reading alone every night. I didn't have to go back to school to get my degree, but it seemed like a useful pursuit. I was only twenty-four, with my whole life ahead of me. The more I could learn about books and their history, the better I could run the store. Besides, it provided me with an opportunity to get out three nights a week.

Now, because of that degree, I was heading out on a new adventure. Mr. Clayton's letter had explained the situation in detail, and it was certainly an interesting one. His uncle, Roland Clayton, had lived on this island, Echo Moon, for the last fifty years or so. He was rich but not too eccentric. Roland had spent his life amassing art, antiques, and books, turning the mansion where he lived into a treasure house of culture.

When Roland died a few months ago, Andrew Clayton, as only living relative, had inherited the lot. Now, on the instructions of his attorney, he wanted an inventory. Would I come to Echo Moon, all expenses paid and with a salary besides, to make some order of Uncle's books?

He collected them, Andrew's letter had said, *but he never put them in any particular order. Quite frankly, Miss Holmes, it will be a monumental task to get the library organized and catalogued.*

Hmm. A challenge. I had liked the sound of it, but it was a week before I wrote back with a list of questions. What was the projected length of the job? Who else would be there? When did I start?

Actually, I'd made up my mind the minute I read the proposal. My more-than-capable assistant manager, Albert, would be delighted to be in charge of the shop while I was gone, and I knew I could trust him not to juggle the books or put rock and roll bands on the Muzak. There was no reason not to take the job.

I had my bags packed before Mr. Clayton — make that Andrew — even replied to my letter.

The drive north had taken me the better part of one day, and it was nearing dinnertime when I finally arrived at the pier where I was to meet the ferry.

Well, it turned out not to be a ferry, exactly. More like an old tugboat. Mostly chipped white paint and creaking boards. At first glance I wondered if the thing would make it the five miles out to the island.

The captain, a gruff, creased-looking man with weathered eyes, met me as I got out of the car.

"Sarah Holmes?" he asked.

I lifted my sunglasses to the top of my head. It was June and still very much daytime at seven P.M.

"Yes. Hello. I'm here to get a ride to Echo Moon Island." I smiled and looked out at the water. Far away, a vague lump sat, small, greenish, hard to distinguish. "Is that it?" I pointed.

"Yes, that's Echo Moon, all right. I'm Bill Packard, miss, and I run the *Molly Jane* to the island and back. We'll have you there in a jiffy."

10

I gave him the car keys, and he quickly removed my luggage from the trunk, then stowed it on board. I lingered next to my car. Now that the moment of parting was upon me, I wasn't at all sure about going. Captain Bill waved to me from the boat, gesturing for me to come aboard. I leaned against the car door and waved back.

"My car!" I shouted so he could hear me. "What about my car?"

He came back down the pier, arms swinging rapidly, shaking his head.

"Well, miss, your car stays put. Won't fit on the boat." He motioned to the *Molly Jane* bobbing lazily back and forth. "And the Claytons don't allow cars on the island, anyhow." He gave a short laugh. "Not that you'd need it. It's just a speck of an island. Bicycles! That's the way to travel on Echo Moon."

I looked at the old gent, tall but potbellied, and imagined him on a ten-speed. You can see I was a bit apprehensive. My nerves were making me giddy.

"I see," I said.

"Now, your car," Captain Bill went on, "we'll just park here in the Claytons' storehouse. It'll be safe. No need to worry about that."

I looked at the looming concrete-block

structure. It certainly looked secure.

Captain Bill drove the car in through the wide garage door, returned my car keys, then silently led the way down the pier to the boat. He helped me onto the tilting deck, then with a hasty smile disappeared into the pilot box. There was a moment of silence; then the rumble of the engine began.

I stood at the back of the boat, wishing I wasn't wearing white. There didn't seem to be any clean places to sit down or lean against, so I stood swaying, watching the mainland drifting away and wondering what was ahead for me on the island called Echo Moon.

Chapter Two

By the time the boat pulled into the dock on the island, I'd worked my way cautiously around to a fairly open area on the starboard side of the *Molly Jane*. With one hand bracing myself, I watched my new place of employment appear and, I must say, it was an impressive sight. The bloom of summer was full upon the island. Lush green trees swayed in the delicate evening breeze. The fading sunlight glinted off the rocks that made up the shore, and in the distance, high on a hill, part of the house could be seen. A Victorian-inspired cupola, complete with weathervane, poked up above the trees. What a view there would be from that room!

I turned my attention back to the dock where Captain Bill was busy securing the boat. A gravel road led away from the shore and back into the woods. As my eyes traced its path, I caught sight of a horse-drawn cart approaching. By squinting, I could see it carried two people. One of them was bound to be Andrew Clayton, I realized in a panic. I hadn't intended to meet him with wind-blown hair and no lipstick. I'd envisioned a formal interview in the library, with a wealthy, distinguished old gent behind a big desk and me in the new deep-purple suit I'd packed so carefully. I'd planned to be cool, composed, and professional. Instead, I was tired, tousled, and casual. At least my sundress had managed to stay clean on the voyage over, even if it was travel creased. *Oh, well,* I thought. *So much for first impressions.*

Captain Bill was intently unloading a bundle of supplies, stacking them onto the dock. I fell into step behind him on one of the trips and followed him down the sagging gangplank onto relatively solid ground. He dropped the pile of boxes he carried next to the others and gave me a smile.

"Good luck, miss, on the job."

Before I even had time to say thank you, the horse cart clattered into view. Bill pointed. "Here comes the boss now, speak of the devil."

The cart creaked to a halt, and I got my first glimpse of Andrew Clayton. "Distinguished old gent" hadn't been quite right. The man leaping nimbly down from the cart wasn't old. He looked about thirty-two. And if "distinguished" implies stuffy, then he wasn't that, either. His tall, stocky frame was attired in a polo shirt that seemed designed to show off well-muscled arms and chinos that were casual but still tailored. His fair hair had a wave just like the one I paid to have installed at the beauty parlor. As he got nearer, I saw bright-blue eyes. Those startling kind that draw you in.

The only part of my errant description that could still apply was "wealthy." He owned this island, so that, at least, must be true. As he approached us, he extended a hand, first to Bill, then to me.

"Welcome to Echo Moon Island, Miss Holmes," he said sincerely, and I had the bizarre urge to curtsy, as if he were the king of somewhere. In a way, I suppose he was.

I said, "It's a pleasure to be here, Mr. Clayton. The island seems lovely."

"Please, make it Andrew." He smiled, white even teeth in a broad grin. "You haven't seen the best of the island yet. Tomorrow morning, first thing, I'll give you a tour."

"That sounds wonderful. I'll look forward to it."

The captain gave a grunt as he hoisted some boxes and ambled off to the cart. Andrew glanced over his shoulder at the seaman loading the supplies onto the cart, and I noticed a faint crescent-shaped scar on his right temple, white against his sun-tanned face. A frown creased his brow and, for an instant, I wondered what the captain had done. Then I realized another man still sat in the cart, holding the horse's reins and staring vacantly off into space.

"Frank!" Andrew's shout startled the old man and he jumped. The look he turned on Andrew was indifferent.

"Yes?" His voice was low and harsh, matching the hardened look of his face. Underneath his battered straw hat, his eyes were barely visible. Faded overalls stretched across his ample middle. He gave every impression of having been recently awakened from a nap.

"Help Bill get the cart loaded. We want to get back to the house soon." Andrew turned back to me with an apologetic smile. "That's Frank Peabody, the caretaker. He's been with Uncle since before I was born. Even though he's slowed down a lot, I've kept him on." We watched as Frank climbed stiffly down and moved slowly to the back of the wagon. He walked with a slight limp, favoring his right leg quite obviously. He joined Bill and halfheartedly began to toss in the boxes.

Andrew dropped his voice to a whisper, although I don't think they could have heard us at that distance. "Truthfully, I'd let him go in an instant. He's turned into a crotchety, domineering, lazy old man." He sighed. "But his wife — Janet — she's a wonder. Like a mother to me, she's been. So, if I want her — and I do — I have to tolerate him!" He jabbed a finger in Frank's direction just as the man looked up. He froze in position, aware of our scrutiny.

I tried to avoid his eyes but couldn't. His angry scowl seemed out of proportion, and I could practically see the sparks of antagonism arc between these two. I shifted nervously from one foot to the other and leaned down to remove a pebble from my sandal. None of this was any of my business. I changed the subject.

"How far is it to the house, Andrew?" I asked.

He turned from his study of Frank and pushed a hand through his hair. "Up this road, it's about half a mile." He pointed in the direction they'd come from. "There's a beautiful winding path that climbs the hill through these woods." Turning to the north, he gestured to where the rocky shore curved out of sight. "There's a sandy beach on the far side of the island. It's in a little cove, so the water is shallow and warm." He smiled at me, and I couldn't help but smile too.

"It's my favorite spot. I hope you packed your swimsuit."

My cheeks felt suddenly flushed, and I bit my lip. "Yes," I said, "I brought it. But I'm really not here for swimming. Tell me about the job ahead."

Andrew led the way over to the horse cart, where the men had finished up and were ready to leave. "Let's talk about that at the house. I need to see the captain now, if you don't mind."

"Not at all," I said.

He handed me up onto the wagon seat and spoke to the caretaker. "Frank, this is Sarah Holmes. She's here to organize the library."

Frank pulled himself onto the seat next to me and gave a grunt that must have been "hello."

Not easily daunted, I held out my hand. "Hello, Mr. Peabody. It's nice to meet you."

His big, callused hand touched mine briefly. "Mm." Not exactly a warm welcome.

"See her back to the house. I'll be along later." Andrew directed his next words to me. "I'm having some remodeling and updating done at the old place. Restoring it to how it was originally but adding a few creature comforts. Actually," he admitted, "Uncle Roland laid out the plans for all the work in his will." He shifted from one foot to the other. "You see, the estate is only mine for my lifetime. After that, after I'm gone, the island, the house, and everything in it goes to the state. Uncle envisioned a museum, and he wanted to make sure it was perfect." He gave a short laugh. "My uncle was a very thorough man, Sarah. He left nothing to chance. The restoration is funded by money left in his will specifically and exclusively for that purpose. You'd think the land meant more to him than I did."

His voice trailed off and I swallowed hard, feeling I'd been given a glimpse of something painful and disturbing.

"I'm sure that wasn't the case," I said reassuringly.

Andrew shook his head. "Well, anyway, watch out for scaffolding and workmen. I shouldn't be long here. Then we'll get down to business."

Frank tapped the reins lightly and made a smooching noise at the big black horse in front of us. With a creak of wagon wheels, we were off.

"Have you lived here on Echo Moon long?" I asked to break the silence.

"Yes. Nearly forty years."

"Wow!" I exclaimed. My head turned this

way and that as we progressed, taking in the heavily wooded scenery. I caught occasional glimpses of squirrels and cottontails in the underbrush. The constant chatter of birds in the branches overhead was like music. "It must be wonderful to live here all year." I sighed. "It's so peaceful."

"Are you from the city, miss?" Frank asked.

"No, not really," I explained. "Greenbrook is a small town. But it seems big compared to this." I gestured around me. "Are we near the house yet?"

"Soon. Another quarter mile or so."

"That's really secluded!"

"It was meant to be," Frank said. Warming to his topic, he went on. "The Clayton family bought the island over one hundred years ago. Mr. Roland's great-great grandfather was with the railroads. Made a fortune watching the tracks laid, then went to live where no tracks could ever reach." He gave a snort of laughter and turned to look at me. "Claytons have lived here ever since." His voice dropped lower, and his eyes turned steely as he added, "No outsiders on Echo Moon, miss. Leastways, none that stayed." For an instant our eyes locked and his message came through as clear as if he'd used a bullhorn.

I swallowed and turned away, looking off into the thinning woods that now gave way to meadows of tall grass.

Frank Peabody didn't want me here. He certainly made no attempts to hide his feelings, and, while his words were not exactly a warning, they were definitely meant to put me off. Of course, I rationalized, I probably wouldn't like intruders, either, if I'd been in the same place for forty years. Like residents of resort towns not liking the "summer people."

All thoughts of Frank fled in an instant, though, as the wagon rounded another corner and the house came into view. It stood three stories. The white exterior needed a good coat of paint, but that in no way detracted from the beauty of the structure. On the lower floor huge, many-paned windows dominated, while the upper-floor windows were framed by big pine-green shutters. High atop the cupola, the weathervane pointed north. Attached to one side of the house was a glass conservatory, and I could see the shadowy green reflection of the plants inside. The work Andrew mentioned must be taking place in back, I figured, as the wagon pulled onto the circle drive in front of the house and stopped at the huge front door. There was no scaffolding that I could see.

Not wanting to spend any more time than necessary with the reticent old caretaker, I slid down from the cart almost before it stopped moving. While I waited, Frank set my bags down on the wide front porch.

"Just go on in, miss. I've got to take these supplies around back." In a flash he was back in the wagon, tapping the reins to start the sturdy horse moving again. The wagon wheels crunched on the gravel path, and the old wagon groaned and creaked as it made its way around the corner of the house and out of sight.

I watched him go with mixed reactions of relief and annoyance. Relief won the brief battle, and I picked up the heavy brass door knocker and let it fall. It clunked heavily. As the sound echoed through the house, I set my shoulders, smoothed my hair, and took a deep breath.

The door was opened almost immediately by a plump, gray-haired woman still wiping her hands on the apron she wore. Mrs. Peabody, I presumed.

"Hello," I said. "I'm —"

"Yes," the elderly woman interrupted, "you're Miss Sarah." Her plump cheeks dimpled. "Please come in." She stepped back and, after retrieving my suitcases from the porch, I followed her inside.

"Oh, dear," Mrs. Peabody said, watching as I set the bags down with a thump. "Frank should have brought those in for you." She shook her head and looked at me with sad eyes. "He's gotten a bit lazy in his old age. Never wants to do anything but putter in the garden these days."

I didn't know how to reply to that and said instead, "You must be Mrs. Peabody. Mr. Clayton told me about you."

"Oh, did he?" she asked. "I'd certainly like to hear what he had to say!" Mrs. Peabody laughed, a warm, cheery sound, and I laughed, too, even though the joke seemed to have slipped by me.

"Let me show you to your room, dear, so you can put those bags away." She turned and walked quickly across the polished wood floor of the entry hall. We marched past gilt-framed watercolors and several glass-fronted display cases filled with tiny treasures to a large oak stairway. The stair railing was topped with a hand-carved wooden pineapple. In the old days the pineapple was a symbol of hospitality, I knew. Thinking of Frank Peabody's odd behavior, I hoped it still was.

The carpeted stair runner was threadbare in the middle, although the fabric along the edges still retained the plush, original texture. The once vibrant colors had become muted over the years. Like the outside of the house, the grandeur of old endured beneath worn surroundings.

Mrs. Peabody kept up a steady stream of chatter as we climbed the stairs and turned right. It took me several seconds to shift my attention from my own ponderings to her conversation.

"I'm so glad Andrew has sent for you, miss. May I call you Sarah? I'm Janet, by the way." She looked over her shoulder at me, lumbering along with my baggage. "We're nearly there, dear. It's the next door on the right."

Out of breath, I could only nod as she went on. "And I think I do a pretty good job of it, if I must say. But Mr. Roland would never let me near that library of his. 'If you get at it, Janet,' he'd say, 'I'll never find a thing.' That room has not had a proper cleaning in ages!" She stopped before a white wooden door at the end of the hall, fished in her skirt pocket for a key, and rattled it in the lock. After pushing the door open, she stood back so I could enter first.

The room was big and, with the curtains against the opposite wall open to the last of the sunlight, quite cheerful.

24

Gratefully I set my bags down next to the old double bed, admiring the elaborate dark-wood headboard. Covering the bed was an obviously handmade quilt, composed of patches of different materials painstakingly sewn together. I ran my hand over the fabric. "This is lovely," I said.

"Well, thank you, Sarah. It's ever so old. Made it when Andrew was just a boy," Janet explained with a pleased smile. She scurried briskly around the room as she spoke. "There's no closet in this room, as you can see. But we do have this armoire." She pointed at the tall wooden chest, opening its doors to show the vast area within. "You must admit, this is prettier than a closet could ever be."

I nodded, looking around the room. All the furnishings had to be antique. That chest, the dresser, the old full-length mirror against one wall. Of course, I reasoned, the Claytons had probably purchased them new.

At the windows, creamy eyelet curtains now hung limp and still, but when the windows were open and the lake breeze wafted in. . . . I could already imagine them dancing about, billowing like sails out on the water.

"I hope you'll be comfortable here. It's a cozy room and, on clear days, the view is just marvelous."

The old lady stood, looking out at the water visible in the distance. Joining Janet at the window, I looked down on some of the meadows and woods we'd driven through and saw the sparkle of the lake beyond. The smooth blue line of the horizon neatly divided water and sky.

"I've never seen so much water in my life!" I exclaimed, laughing. "My hometown is landlocked. We've got rivers and creeks and a lake, of sorts. You can see both sides of it, though, and in dry summers walk all the way across with the water just up to your waist."

"It's a grand sight," Janet agreed. "Moody, though, you know." She turned to look up at me. She was all of five feet, and I'm five foot eight, so it was a bit of a stretch. Her blue eyes sparkled intently, and I could tell she really believed what she said. "Cheery and bright some days. Black and gloomy on others. Just like a person. . . ."

Her voice trailed off, and we stood silently for a moment, viewing the lake.

Coming back from her daydream, Janet said, "I'm sure you'd like to freshen up after your trip. The bathroom is just across the hall." She gestured in that direction and started toward the door. "Mr. McDownell, the antiques man, also has a room in this wing, so you'll have to share it, I'm afraid."

I smiled, charmed by her almost Victorian attitude. "I'm sure that will be fine."

"Andrew has his room in the other wing, of course," she prattled on, ticking off names on her fingers. "Frank and I have a suite just off the kitchen. I'll show you when you come downstairs. Those workmen of Mr. McDownell's are staying in the cottage out back." She shook her head as she opened the door to leave. "Plenty of room in the house, but they said no, they'd be just as happy off by themselves. Guess I'll never understand men!" With a wave of one hand, she was gone.

As I began unpacking, hanging my clothes in the big armoire and storing socks and underthings in the cedar-scented dresser drawers, I thought about Janet and her friendly, open manner. "If strangers aren't welcome on Echo Moon Island," I said to my mirrored reflection across the room, "someone forgot to tell her. She's made me feel right at home!"

Chapter Three

A short time later, after I'd combed the tangles from my hair and renewed my makeup — two things guaranteed to revive the weary traveler — I made my way back downstairs. I had changed into a turquoise floral-print skirt and simple white cotton blouse and pulled my shoulder-length hair back into a tiny ponytail. Most of the year my hair is decidedly brown and refuses to take a curl. In the summer the sun turns it a rather nice shade of auburn, and the humidity brings out waves that seem to exist just between Memorial Day and Labor Day. Before I'd left my room, I'd used the mirror for a full appraisal and had approved the summer's changes. My spirits rose and I confidently went searching for Janet.

As I descended the staircase, I took in the deserted scene below. I resisted the urge to think of the sight before me as a drawing room, but that was the term that came to mind. A huge fireplace took up most of the wall opposite the window. Faded floral rugs were scattered about the wooden floors. A rolltop desk, standing against one wall, sported a green-shaded brass lamp. An upright piano, complete with metronome, rounded out the furnishings. From the ceiling hung an old chandelier. It was not fancy crystal but carved wood, with elaborately twisted stems ending in six sockets. Idly, I wondered where Andrew's ancestors had found such a singular creation and made a mental note to ask him.

Speaking of whom, I thought, where could he be? He had said at the dock he would be along soon, so he must be in the house. Surely Janet would know where I could find him. I turned away from the stairs and headed down the hall, poking my head into the rooms. I wasn't really snooping. I was just curious.

One room simply had to be the ladies' parlor, judging from the pastel color scheme and rococo "wedding cake" ceiling. In the gloom of twilight, my overactive imagination could easily picture Edwardian ladies perched on the delicate chairs, their hands busy with needlepoint, their quiet laughter gracing the air. I gave a romantic sigh and moved on.

Along the hallway many portraits hung, and I couldn't help wondering who the people were as I stopped to take a look. One sepia photograph was of a family gathering. The women all wore straw boaters on their upswept hair. Their long dark skirts were topped with full-sleeved white blouses. With the water of the lake in the background, it made quite a nautical scene. The men were also dressed in the severe fashion of the day, with hair slicked back and mustaches waxed into handlebar shapes.

"There you are!" Janet Peabody's voice startled me from my thoughts. "Let me show you the rest of the house; then we'll have some tea. I'm afraid dinner is served early in this house, but there is always plenty left over."

I explained I'd had dinner just before arriving and tea would be more than enough. Then, with me hiding a smile, the energetic housekeeper showed me the rooms I'd already seen, and plenty of ones I hadn't gotten to yet.

The music room was the current scene of restoration and improvement. The intricate molded ceiling was being reworked and the walls repainted. Huge plastic drop cloths covered the spectacular mosaic floor.

As we continued our tour, I realized the truth of Andrew's words. When he described his uncle as a collector, he had not exaggerated. Beautiful art pieces — paintings, sculpture, and engravings — decorated the hall-ways, the walls, and the tabletops. The inlaid wood-and-glass cabinet near the doorway in the dining room contained a positively stun-ning collection of Oriental netsuke. The tiny, carved ivory pieces seemed to glow from within, each miniature figurine an original and priceless work of art.

"Oh, yes. Mr. Roland was quite a con-noisseur, you know," Janet explained, run-ning her hand over a marble statue displayed inconspicuously on the sideboard. "Most of the things in the house are his, although his father was a bit of an expert too. Mr. Ro-land's specialty was books, of course. His first love." She paused and gave me a con-spiratorial wink. "Yours, too, hmm?"

"Well, yes, actually," I agreed, following behind as she led the way out of one room and back down the hallway that divided the house.

"Time you saw the library, then," Janet stated. "I've been saving that for last be-cause I know once you see it, you'll want to stay there a while."

The double doors to the library were glass. The curtains on the inside prevented me from seeing in until a key had once more been produced and the doors were pushed open.

Standing in the doorway, I was filled with awe and delight as I surveyed the room. Floor-to-ceiling bookcases outlined the room on two sides. Under the windows, looking out to the garden, more shelves squatted, spilling books over their edges and onto the floor. In the middle of the room sat a huge wooden desk, piled high with papers and more books. Freestanding bookcases stood in rows like public-library stacks. The architectural details of the room were completely hidden beneath the mountain of volumes.

Turning my dazzled eyes to Janet's amused face, I let out a long whistle. "Good grief! It's as big as the university library!"

Janet laughed and patted my arm. "Well, don't despair. Andrew will give you plenty of time to get your project done."

"Despair?" I shook my head. "No, it's wonderful. A little overwhelming, I'll admit. But what fun it will be to turn this" — I searched for a tactful phrase and couldn't find one — "this jumbled mess into orderly, Dewey-decimaled shelves!" Inspired, I drifted into the room, spreading my arms out as if to gather it all in at once.

"Why don't you stay here and have a look around while I go get the tea?" Janet suggested.

I'm afraid the nod I gave was distracted. I'd been totally entranced by my surroundings and wandered now from shelf to shelf, occasionally tripping over a stack of books left carelessly on the floor. Perusing the titles, I wondered where to start. The Old Curiosity Shop had never looked like this!

Eventually I reached the desk in the middle of the room. A sturdy, carved-wood Victorian model, it was built to withstand a beating. *And that's just what it has taken,* I thought, removing the piles of books that crowded its surface.

"I'll need room to work," I muttered, shifting books from the desk top to the floor. As I lifted off the last of the load, I felt the desk wobble. Without the heavy books holding them in place, the uneven legs caused a definite jiggle.

"Hmm." I knelt down to examine the legs and easily determined which one caused the trouble. I had just scrambled back out from beneath the desk and pushed on its surface once more when the library door opened.

Without looking up, I said, "Janet, this desk needs a leg repaired. Do you think Frank could fix it? It jiggles. See?" I pressed on the top and frowned as the desk seesawed.

When Janet didn't answer, I glanced up

and blushed scarlet. It was not Mrs. Peabody who stood before me, but a man I'd never seen before. "Oh, I'm sorry," I apologized, glad to see the tall, dark-haired man smiling. "I didn't realize —" I broke off lamely. My mistake was obvious.

"Well, I must say, I've never been taken for a little old lady before," he said, crossing the room to join me.

At over six feet, with broad shoulders and sinewy arms quite apparent beneath the button-down shirt he wore, I could certainly believe his statement. He looked fit and sturdy. The creases at the corners of his eyes made me guess him to be about thirty-five. Who could he be?

"I'm Sarah Holmes." I extended my hand. "Librarian."

He took it in a warm, firm clasp. "Richard McDownell. Antiques."

I held his gaze for a long moment, our eyes battling each other. My gray against his deep brown. I saw humor in his look, thank goodness. When I blinked, the concentration broke.

"I have a problem with this desk," I explained unnecessarily, turning to the object in question. "It wobbles."

"So I heard." Richard was already leaning over to size up the trouble. He straightened, his eyes scanning the nearest pile of dusty old books. "Until Frank can find time to fix this properly, this should do." In his hand was a small, thin volume. The fabric at the top of the spine was frayed. No doubt the inside pages also showed their years.

Richard lifted the desk and slid the book under the offending leg. "Problem solved. Temporarily," he said.

I laughed. "You're a genius," I joked. "I could have done that."

Richard's smile remained as he tapped his index finger against his temple. "Yes. But I did!"

I shook my head, liking this stranger and his take-charge attitude. No nonsense, no delays. Just action. Admirable traits, in my book.

When I pushed on the desk top, it remained steady. "Well, thank you, anyway. I have a feeling that if I asked Frank Peabody, I'd wait a good long while." I frowned, confessing in a rush, "I don't think he likes me."

"Oh, him." Richard waved a hand in dismissal. He perched on the corner of the desk. "I've been here two weeks, and he still hasn't said a word to me. Bobs his head when I say hello, but that's it. I don't think he likes anyone."

"But, Janet — Mrs. Peabody — is so friendly!"

"If you had to live alone on an island with Frank, wouldn't you welcome a distraction too?" he asked.

I laughed, shuddering comically at the very thought.

Richard's eyes traveled rapidly over me, and I squirmed under the scrutiny. "And you make quite a distraction, I must say."

A blush flooded my cheeks, part embarrassment, part anger. He was no-nonsense all right. He got straight to the point. I'd never found it easy to accept a compliment and, at the same time, resented being trivially placed in the pigeonhole marked "pretty girl."

"Let's hope that isn't true," I said matter-of-factly, "because we both have plenty of work to do." I turned away from him and scanned the huge, cluttered room. "I don't even know where to start!"

"Don't start now!" Janet called from the library door. She pushed a tea trolley toward us. "I see you met Richard. He's the antiques man." She poured three glasses of iced tea with lemon and handed them around. The mention of antiques got her started on a trip down memory lane, and we listened politely to her stories of days gone by.

Her former employer, Roland Clayton, had obviously been very important to Janet and her husband.

"Didn't you ever get lonely here on the island?" I asked, helping myself to another delicious sugar cookie from the heaping plate Janet held out.

She sipped her drink before answering. "Sometimes, I will say, it would have been nice to have another female around." She turned to Richard and explained. "For girl talk, you know. But most times I've been quite content. Echo Moon has been my home for so long, I can't imagine ever living anywhere else."

She'd gotten a far-off look in her eye, lost in the past. Richard and I exchanged a long look.

He looked down at his watch. "Well, Mrs. Peabody, thank you so much for the tea." He glanced out the window at the deepening shadows. "I've got some paperwork to catch up on before tomorrow, so I think I'll say good night."

I followed his glance out the window and was surprised to find that night had fallen. Seeing the darkness made me feel suddenly tired. It had been a long, busy day. "I think I'll just turn in too," I said, gathering up the glasses and returning them to the cart.

"Do you need any help?"

Janet shook her head. "No, no, dear. You two run along. It is rather late at that. I'm surprised Frank hasn't come looking for me already." She pushed the cart to the door and let us go past into the hall. The library doors were then closed and locked.

"Here," she said, handing me the key with some ceremony. "Since you are in charge now, you'd better have this. Mr. Roland was quite adamant that the library always be kept locked. So, please, see that it is."

I nodded. "I'll remember."

"Good, then. And good night to you both." She pushed the cart off down the hall, humming very faintly to herself.

We climbed the staircase together as Richard asked, "We're in the same wing, right?"

"Yes." I looked around the quiet house. The stairs creaked beneath our feet. Shadows filled every corner. "It's nice to know there will be someone just across the hall."

When we reached my door, Richard leaned against the wall, one hand resting on the doorframe. "Don't tell me you're afraid of ghosts!"

"Ghosts!" The word exploded from my lips. "Janet never mentioned any ghosts."

"Yes, but a house this old just looks like it must harbor a few, doesn't it?"

My smile was shaky as I answered. "Thanks to that remark, I won't sleep a wink all night." I opened the door and stepped inside. "See you in the morning."

He bobbed his head. "Good night."

I waited until I heard his door close before bolting my own. Could there really be ghosts? I wondered, heading toward the dresser and kicking my shoes into the corner of the room.

It was as I was putting my jewelry onto the dresser top that I saw the note. It rested up against a tiny bronze art deco figurine. Printed on a plain piece of paper in big block letters, it said: *LEAVE ECHO MOON AT ONCE. YOU ARE IN DANGER.*

For a moment I stood frozen, the silence around me making a rushing in my ears like the sound of the sea. Then I whirled around, my eyes searching the room, as if the person who left the message would still be there. Of course, no one was. My heart thumped heavily, and my hands were shaking as I sank down onto the bed.

Questions shot through my mind, all demanding answers when I had none. Why was I being told to get out? Who had left the note for me? One of Richard's "ghosts" or Frank Peabody? I'd been out of my room for several hours. Anyone could have entered, delivered a message and gone, with me none the wiser. Rubbing my tired eyes with both hands, I wondered: What was going on here?

I took a deep breath and clenched my hands together, collecting my thoughts and my nerve. Gingerly fingering the note, thinking about fingerprints and television detective shows, I reread the few words. Now I was more confused than frightened. Was it a threat or a warning? Was someone trying to protect me or scare me?

Nervously I paced the room, my arms crossed over my chest to ward off a chill that had nothing to do with the weather. The bedroom curtains hadn't been drawn, and I stood looking out into the black of night. There was just a faint suggestion of moonlight filtering from behind the clouds, turning the lake into smooth, silver ice. The scene was beautiful and serene, and yet all was not as it seemed, I knew.

But the mysteries of the evening were not over yet.

As I stood sentinel, leaning my head against the window frame, I saw a flash of light. Not in the sky, so it couldn't be lightning or a plane overhead. No, it was lower, in the woods. My eyes strained to penetrate the dark, and the flash came again. Just opposite my room, down in the woods, someone was walking.

And watching?

Chapter Four

Thump!

The stack of books I carried joined the others already piled on the floor near the library windows. I rose slowly, one hand pressing into the ache in the small of my back.

"Lift with your legs, not with your back," I muttered in discontent, "and you still end up sore."

I'd spent most of the morning in the library, doing preliminary sorting. It was a good job for right now because, not only was it an important first step, but it also gave me time to ponder the events of the night before.

I hadn't really expected to sleep a wink after the nerve-rattling note, the light in the woods, and Richard's silly talk of ghosts. But the body has a mind of its own, and once I was tucked into the big double bed, I'd dropped right off into a heavy, dreamless sleep. Of course, I'd pulled the curtains over the window, after making certain it was locked. I'd even dragged the straight-back chair across the room and jammed it firmly under the doorknob.

That had made for a rather embarrassing moment in the morning when Janet had knocked on the door with early-morning tea. She had had to wait in the hall while I wrestled the heavy chair back into place. Sheepishly I'd unlocked and opened the door.

Janet had a puzzled look on her face, one that made her eyes crinkle up and her lips purse. Still, to her credit, she didn't say a word. I took the tray and thanked her, sipping the steaming tea while she yanked open the curtains with an energetic flair, throwing wide the sash to let in the morning breeze.

Sometime in the night my subconscious had made the decision not to mention my note to anyone. Since I had no idea who had sent it or why, it would be silly to babble about it to everyone in sight. It was clear the message was meant to be a secret.

As far as the light in the woods went, well, with the clear sunshine of day, my suspicion over that seemed a bit over-dramatic. Maybe Frank had been out for a walk. Maybe Andrew Clayton had. People went fishing at night sometimes, didn't they? It could have been caused by any number of perfectly reasonable things. I had no desire to be branded "hysterical," at least not without justification, and considered the incidents over.

Still, it hadn't been easy at the breakfast table. When Richard greeted me with a warm smile and asked, "How are you this morning?" part of me wanted to sit right down and tell him everything. He was one of those people you meet and instantly feel you know.

But I didn't know him. Not really. As much as I disliked the idea, I had to admit Richard, too, had had plenty of opportunity to sneak into my room with the frightening missive. So, I'd made some lighthearted remark and joined him at the table.

His two workmen, known to me only as Chuck and Joe, had also been there. The Peabodys ate in their own quarters apparently. Andrew had not yet come down. Richard had explained to me a bit of what they were hoping to accomplish in the music room, and I found it fascinating. Andrew wanted the room to look exactly as it had when first built, with elaborate paintings over the huge, arched doorways, molded ceiling designs, heavy floral wallpaper, and restored mosaic tiling on the floor.

"It would help," Richard said, "if we had some original photographs of the room." He spread marmalade on toast and ate a bite before continuing. "Right now we're going from period illustrations, using what was usual and common as decoration. To do a really good job, though, would require original details."

I sipped my coffee and thought. "You have no photos of the house?" I asked.

Richard shrugged. "Apparently there were some, but not of that room. At least, none that have turned up. In my past experience the only other place we've ever found the kinds of facts we're looking for has been in letters, diaries, and journals. The womenfolk would send descriptions of their new places to relatives. If they were detailed enough, it gives us everything we need to know."

I speared a piece of grapefruit and regarded it thoughtfully. "Maybe I'll find some of that information in the library." I shrugged. "I don't know if Roland Clayton kept his family's personal papers there, but it would seem a logical spot."

Richard nodded. "Well, keep an eye peeled," he requested. "We'd certainly be grateful."

I thought of our discussion now as I surveyed the library. After all my work, the room didn't actually look much better, but I knew the beginnings of organization were there. During my excavation I'd found a few old ledgers, but no diaries or photo albums. I hadn't really taken the time to even look at the books, but just set them aside to glance through later.

That was now.

Deciding a break was in order, I picked up the oversized volumes and headed across the room to the big open windows. As I sidestepped mounds of unsorted books, my thoughts drifted back to the Old Curiosity Shop and its neat, tidy appearance. Would this room ever look that way? I looked around, trying to see the place with a professional eye, imagining the orderly shelves and rearranged room.

Two comfortable armchairs near the windows would catch the summer breeze and make an excellent haven for the reader. Thinking of the future scene, I stepped to the big windows, pushing them open still farther, feeling the cool lake breeze against my skin. This side of the house faced one of the formal gardens, and the breeze brought with it the scent of many flowers in bloom. The broad sill was deep enough to qualify as a window seat, and I settled right in, curling my legs up underneath me, breathing deeply of the sweet-smelling air.

It was easy to forget that someone didn't

want me here. It was easy to pretend I'd lived here always. Echo Moon seemed to be a place for daydreams — and for nightmares.

Dismissing the thought, I opened the dusty cover of the first ledger on my lap. As I'd suspected, it was a household-accounts book. Faded, spidery writing filled every line in methodical fashion. Whoever had kept the books had done a good job. Without much interest, I flipped the brittle pages. Maybe Richard could find something useful in these, but it didn't seem likely.

I leafed rapidly through a few more books, coming at last to the one that looked most recent. The cover was still intact. When I opened it, I saw at once this had been done by a different hand, in ballpoint, not fountain pen. The words on the first page gave me a jolt:

Library inventory. Fall, 1986.

A firm handwriting filled the pages that followed with titles, copyright notations, and remarks on the condition of the books. Outside my window the birds sang gently from their homes in the trees, and the leaves swayed in the wind, rustling against each other in a sound quite similar to that of waves breaking on the shore. But I missed it all.

Delighted over my find, I looked with admiration at the painstakingly detailed account. I thought of the hours of work Roland Clayton had put into his collection, for who else but the collector would be so precise, would add notations as to where the books were obtained and for how much?

I didn't even look up when the door opened across the room. Unaware that my boss had come in, I read a few more pages, my head propped on my chin.

"Well, you look comfortable." His voice sounded more than a little amused.

I'm afraid I jumped, startled out of my contemplation of the entry *"Historian's History of Western Civilization* (gift from the old girl)."* My first thought was, What old girl? My second was, Jump to attention! Slipping rapidly from my window perch, I closed the book and dropped it on the sill.

"Just taking a breather," I explained. "I've been busy this morning. Look!" My hands spread to emphasize my accomplishment, and I gave Andrew a quick synopsis of my plan of attack.

Today he wore deep-blue shorts and a blue-and-white knit shirt, the buttons open at the neck. He looked casual and comfortable, making me realize how disheveled I must look after toting books and sitting on the floor to sort them. As if he could read my mind, Andrew said, "You have a smudge. Right here." His index finger touched my cheek and traced the streak to my chin.

I swallowed and stepped away, suddenly warm. Wiping rapidly at the spot, I explained, "Some of the books are very dusty." I smiled weakly, avoiding his eyes. "Before I'm finished, they'll all be properly cleaned."

Andrew nodded briskly. "I'm sure they will, Sarah. You strike me as a hardworking person."

This was just the image I wanted him to have, of course, but his tone seemed a bit sarcastic. He picked one of the books off a shelf and turned it over, running his hand absently across the cover.

"I promised you a tour of the island yesterday. Remember?"

I nodded and he continued. "If you can tear yourself away, we could go this afternoon. How does that sound?"

Truthfully, all I wanted to do was get my hands on that inventory book and start matching volumes to the entries, but I could see that would have to wait.

"Yes, that would be perfect," I said in a hearty, enthusiastic tone. "Do you want to leave right now?"

We agreed to meet in half an hour's time in front of the house. On my way upstairs I detoured past the music room.

A portable radio sat on the floor, tuned to an easy-listening station. Redheaded Chuck perched high on a ladder, working on the ceiling motifs. Joe and Richard had their heads together across the room, conferring on something.

I knocked on the doorjamb, and all three turned. "Richard, do you have a minute?" I asked.

He gave a brisk nod, left Joe holding a sheaf of papers, and came over to me.

"What can I do for you, Marian-the-Librarian?" he asked with a grin.

I smiled. I'd been a fan of *The Music Man* for years and recognized the reference. When I told Richard of the household-account books I had turned up, he beamed, obviously excited at the prospect.

"I honestly don't think they will be very useful," I cautioned. "But you would know that better than I."

He dismissed my skepticism. "Hidden treasure," he said. "Every little bit helps. It could save me a lot of research time if I find what we need."

Nodding, I told him of my other lucky find — the library inventory. "It should really help with cataloging," I said. "Although it does seem odd that Roland went to such trouble with record keeping and still allowed his books to be so unorganized." I pressed my lips together and thought. "You'd expect someone so meticulous to be that way consistently."

Richard shrugged. "I'm not so sure. Not all collections are meant to be sealed under glass for posterity. He probably enjoyed reading the books. Using them regularly and, as a result, messing them up."

I suppose he had a point, but it still didn't seem to follow.

"You know" — Richard's voice dropped low, and I leaned closer to catch his next words — "I have a similar listing for his paintings." My eyes widened. "Found it with the blueprints of the house. I haven't had the chance or the need to use it yet, but eventually, as work here progresses, it should be quite handy."

One of the workmen dropped a tool, and it clattered heavily behind us.

"Watch out, there!" Richard called good-naturedly. Then he said to me, "I'd better get back to work. Could I see those books later?"

I nodded and suggested that evening after dinner.

51

"Sounds great." Richard took a step away. "See you later. And thanks again." He punctuated the last by winking, and I bit back a smile, looking forward to our next meeting.

As I changed clothes, I thought about Richard and realized that I could easily become interested in him. Here we were sharing a common goal — the restoration of Roland Clayton's estate — and spending idyllic summer days on a beautiful island. I ran the brush through my hair and nearly laughed out loud at the picture my thoughts conjured up. A tropical-island paradise with the two of us sipping cool drinks out of coconut shells suited my romantic daydream. Reality, however, was quite different.

Shaking my head to dispel the cobwebs, I forced myself to concentrate on the here and now. Already Andrew must be outside waiting for me. I laced up my sneakers and took a quick glance in the mirror. He had told me to dress for a bike ride, and so I had, in pink-and-white-striped shorts and a white terry T-shirt. At the last minute I thought to grab a cloth-covered rubber band to pull back my hair.

When I got downstairs, Andrew was there, standing between two big old bicycles. He had his back to me but turned as I approached and gave me an appreciative glance.

"Ready to ride?" he asked.

I looked at the ancient balloon-tire bikes and nodded. At home I spent summers getting around on a ten-speed with tires as wide as a watchband and a seat to match. Old bikes, like old cars, were built for comfort and not speed, so I expected a leisurely ride today.

We climbed aboard and, with Andrew leading the way, coasted off down the gravel drive. The first part of the trip was familiar as we followed the horse path through the woods and past the dock where just yesterday the *Molly Jane* had lolled.

After that it was all new to me, and I kept close to Andrew so I wouldn't miss anything. The path we took was right at the water's edge, with just a shoreline of smooth, white rocks separating us from the lake.

"This is the trail that runs all around the island's coast," Andrew explained. "But it's just one of many paths. The entire island is crisscrossed by them."

The one we rode on was made from crushed limestone, making pedaling fairly effortless and leaving a faint cloud of dust rising behind us into the dry summer air.

The other trails, Andrew said, were sand or dirt.

I thought of riding this heavy old bike uphill in sand and grimaced. Talk about aerobics!

After we had gone a half mile or so, the path curved sharply, forming a horseshoe-shaped cove. I knew immediately it must be the beach he had spoken of earlier. The sunlight danced off the deep-blue water and set it twinkling like snow in the moonlight. My feet slowed of their own accord as I took a deep breath, gazing around me in something close to awe.

"What a perfect spot!" I declared when we coasted to a stop, pulling off the trail onto the soft, warm sand.

Andrew laughed, swinging one tanned, muscular leg off his bike and letting its kick-stand sink into the moist sand.

I parked my bike next to his and went to join him at the water's edge. He stood with both hands on his hips, looking for all the world like the King of Siam. Proud, confident, secure. I kicked off my shoes and let my toes press down, making little valleys in the soft surface. For several moments we stood in a companionable silence, admiring the unbroken view of the lake.

At last Andrew gave a deep sigh. "This

island has been in my family for generations," he said with emotion. "No matter how many valuables Uncle Roland and Granddad and all the Claytons before them accumulated, no matter how many millions they were worth, this" — he turned to spread his arms wide, as if to gather up the island, the cove, and the sky — "this is the most important one. It's priceless!"

I nodded, easily able to understand his feelings. "Do you live here all year with the Peabodys?" I asked, suddenly realizing that I knew virtually nothing about my employer other than what his letter had told me, and all that had related to the library.

His fair hair shook, shifting back and forth with the movement of his head. "Oh, no," he said. "Maybe that's why it is so special to me now. I grew up on the island, with Uncle Roland. My parents were killed when I was just a baby. There was no one else to take care of me, so Uncle took me in. Except for school, I didn't leave here until college. These days, I only get up here on the weekends." He turned away from me, and some of the brightness seemed to dim from his attitude. "Of course, I'm planning to stay this summer. I own a real-estate business in South Clifton, but I've shut it down for a few months. Getting an estate in order is very time-consuming, you know. Uncle's only been gone for about six months, and this is the first chance I've had to start straightening things out."

Judging from the looks of the library, I thought, *it needs a lot of that.* I said, "I didn't know you had a business." It was hard to picture him in a suit and tie. Since I'd only seen him in casual clothes, that was the way I always imagined him. Still, he was an attractive man, energetic and fit, with only the slightest suggestion of extra flesh around the middle. Dressed up, he could be quite a stunner. I looked over at him, watching his profile — jutting chin, squared off and firm; sturdy, sloping nose beneath blue eyes; bushy brows, knit now in thought.

"Huh?" Obviously his mind had been on other things, and I repeated my remark.

"Oh, yes. I started it up about five years ago." He leaned down and picked up a smooth flat rock. He ran his thumb over it several times, using it as a worry stone. "Uncle was very helpful at the time. He gave me the initial capital. Even engaged a market analyst to help select the location. It was worth it." He flung his arm out to the side, sending the stone skipping and pitching over the water time after time before it disappeared beneath the surface. "It's going great guns."

I picked up a stone of my own and imitated his movement. A tiny splash of water shot straight up as the rock sank with only a ripple. I laughed. Even as a child I hadn't mastered this skill. Some things never change.

Andrew laughed too, offering lessons if I ever wanted to learn proper technique.

"That doesn't strike me as an essential life skill," I teased, declining.

Together we walked back to our bikes and soon were back on the path, which was now about thirty feet from the water's edge. The area on each side was filled with trees, dappling the sunlight and casting welcome shade onto the trail. It was an abrupt change from the bright beach, suddenly dark and cool. A shiver danced swiftly up my spine, and I shook my shoulders to drive it off.

We started climbing then, and I pedaled with effort, standing up on the bike and gripping the handlebars tight. Ahead of me, Andrew puffed along, his conversation coming in little gasps.

"The grade lasts . . . just a short way. . . . Then we'll be at . . . the island's highest point. . . . There's a tower. . . ." He gave up talking and motioned to the right. I could just see the bottom of whatever tower he referred to.

We grunted up the last of the hill to the big wooden base of the structure, and I craned my neck to look up. It was a look-out tower, like the ones in state parks. It loomed up at least one hundred feet, with observation decks at various heights along the way.

After we caught our breath, Andrew explained. "It was built for watching ships come in, I guess. No one is really too sure. Uncle always called it 'Granddad's Folly,' but then, Uncle was afraid of heights."

We laughed together and took a stroll around the heavy legs to where the stairs began. Andrew gamely went up the first few. I sagged against the handrail and watched him climb. My hair had slipped from its ponytail, and I pushed it limply off my face. I was warm from exertion. Tired too. My legs rebelled at the very thought of climbing who-knew-how-many steps and, of their own accord, gently collapsed beneath me so I sat on the bottom step.

It took Andrew about ten seconds to realize I was not behind him, and he soon reappeared. Exposure to the afternoon sun had brought a flush to his face, making the white crescent at his temple more noticeable. His nose was beginning to glow with sunburn, and I figured mine probably was too.

"Aren't you coming?" he asked.

Shaking my head, eyes wide, I said, "Are you kidding? Only if you carry me!"

He folded those long legs and sat on a step about five feet above me. "I know you're thin, Sarah, but I don't think I'm up to that," he teased.

"I'd like to see the top someday, Andrew. The view must be stunning!"

He nodded. "Yes. Like everything here, it's remarkable. We'll save it for our next trip," he promised. "If you've got any energy left, we could stop at the berry patch for a quick snack." When I looked puzzled, he went on. "Several kinds of berries grow wild on the island. All over it, actually. But there's one spot in particular, not far from here, where the biggest ones grow."

My throat was dry, and the thought of a juicy berry made my mouth water. I pulled myself up. "Lead the way."

He was right. It wasn't far, and in no time we were picking the black and red berries and gobbling them up. They were warm from the sunshine and gritty against my teeth. The juice was sweet and wonderful.

"Have you seen enough for one day?"

Andrew asked, handing me an especially plump blackberry.

"I think my body could use a rest, I'll admit. What I've seen is beautiful, and I'd like to see more another time."

"Of course." He bent a high branch down to us, and we pulled off more of the fruit.

"I'm anxious to get back to work," I said, not to butter up the boss but because I really meant it.

"Oh, really?" He sounded doubtful.

"Yes." I couldn't keep the excitement from my voice as I remembered my morning discovery. "I found an inventory of the library your uncle must have done in 1986. It lists all the books and appears to be very thorough. It should prove really useful in my work. What a lucky thing!"

I beamed over at him, but he didn't beam back. His face had gone blank, and I wondered if he'd even heard me.

"Well, that's good," he said, bobbing his head absently. "An inventory. I never knew Uncle did that." His eyes focused and looked piercingly at me. "Where did you say you found it?"

"In the library. On one of the shelves." The words almost came out as a question. I wondered if I'd said the wrong thing, even mentioning the ledger. But what could be wrong with having a complete list of volumes? "Would you like to see it?" I offered.

Andrew ate another berry and held his cupped palm out to me. I took another one too. "No, Sarah. I have no interest in any of the technical stuff. That's why you're here." His smile returned, wide and white. "You just fix it all up and tell me when you're done." He gulped the last of the fruit in his hand and dusted his palms off, the cheery host once more.

"Next stop, home!" he said and we pointed our bikes south, completing our circle tour of Echo Moon.

Chapter Five

I reached into my pocket for the key to the library door. Richard and I had hurried through Janet's delicious apple-cobbler dessert and were ready for a long look at the household-account books. I'd revived from the bike trip by taking a refreshing shower, followed by a catnap. Now, with Richard standing behind me holding our coffee cups, I felt around in the pocket of the skirt I'd worn that morning. Then I felt again, rapidly, anxiously. The key was gone!

I must have gone white because Richard said quickly, "What's wrong?"

I hardly heard him. My mind was busy racing over my actions when I'd left the library earlier. Had I locked the door? Could I have forgotten such an important thing?

"I've lost the key!" I said at last, looking at Richard and willing him to produce it from behind his ear. Anything to keep me from having to admit such carelessness to Janet and to Andrew.

"Are you sure?" He looked puzzled but

not overly concerned. "Maybe you forgot it inside?"

I shook my head and sputtered angrily as he set the coffee cups down on the nearby marble-topped table in the hall and went to try the door.

"Don't be ridiculous! Of course I locked it. I remember doing it. And I put the key right here in my pocket." I pointed at the pocket, inside out and empty. "After the way Janet went on about it, I'd never —"

The doorknob turned easily under Richard's hand and, wordlessly, he let it swing inward. Our eyes met and I knew he thought I was either stupid or crazy.

I followed him into the dark room, carrying our cups. "I'm not stupid, Richard! And I'm not crazy. I know I locked that door!"

He turned on the light switch and closed the door behind me. "No one else has to know about this," he said. "I wouldn't want you to get in any trouble."

Exasperated, I set the cups down on the desktop with a bang. If he didn't want to believe me, I certainly couldn't make him. Not without proof. "Let's just forget it," I said. "But I still don't have the key."

Richard sipped his coffee. "In your room?" he suggested.

I started to deny it again, then stopped. Maybe it was in my room. I wasn't sure anymore. "I'll have to check later," I said. "Let me show you these books." He joined me near the window while the twilight began in the garden beyond.

As I watched, Richard flipped the fragile, yellowed pages, looking for any details relating to the music room. Several times his brows came together and I saw him fingering the corner of a page. Before long we were both going through the books, our eyes slowly deciphering the faded writing. Richard found a notebook I'd brought down earlier and began taking notes, jotting down page numbers for further study. It reminded me of my college days, doing research in the big stacks of the university library. I'd spent hours there, over the years, and remembered well the feel of a book in my hand, knowing if I looked hard enough and in just the right place, I'd find the answers to my questions.

After an hour or more had passed, Richard let out a cry, startling me in the silence. "Aha!" His finger tapped the page, and he looked at me with shining eyes.

I leaned closer to read the words, then looked at him again. "It's an order for wallpaper," I said, wondering what was so exciting about that.

He nodded. "It could be music-room wallpaper!" For a moment the idea hung in the air.

"And then again, it couldn't," I felt obliged to point out. "How will you ever know?"

In high spirits, Richard twirled an imaginary mustache and put on a German accent. "Ve have vays, my dear."

I laughed, caught up in his excitement. Suddenly, without warning, his lips touched mine. Just for an instant. In fact, it was over so fast, I wondered if I'd imagined that too. But one look at his face told me I hadn't.

His warm, dark eyes seemed lit from within, and my heart began to race. Carefully he set the book down on the floor, took my book from my hands, and put it out of harm's way as well. Then, turning to me, he placed his hands over mine, holding them gently in a warm and pleasant grasp. I was aware of the sounds of the garden — the birds, the crickets, the leaves caught in the breeze. The setting sun's last rays turned the room gold, emphasizing his tan, bringing a glow to his face, so near mine.

I closed my eyes as he drew me closer. When he kissed me, I thought of the blackberries — soft, warm, sweet, and wonderful.

Deep inside me, bells were ringing, in joy and in warning. I heard only the joyous one and relaxed in Richard's arms, willing the kiss to go on and on.

"Mmmm." Richard gently released my lips and tenderly placed another kiss on my forehead.

I put my hands against his chest, feeling the strength of his muscles beneath the light cotton shirt.

"I told you you were a distraction," he teased.

I remembered his earlier words with a smile. It wasn't exactly easy for me to keep my mind on books with these marvelous interruptions.

"I guess we'll have to work around it," I said, holding his hand in both of mine and absently noting the squared nails, callused spots, and minor abrasions of this working-man's hand.

"We should be working now," he reminded me and I sighed. It was true. I was collecting a salary, and I should be earning it, not kissing men I'd only known for two days.

"Right," I agreed and we returned to our reading, sitting close together.

A while later Richard set aside the last of the account books and turned to face me.

"Do you have any more?"

"No." I shook my head. I glanced around the big, mostly jumbled library. "I've only been on the job one day, after all, and this is a big place. Maybe I'll find more."

"Yes." Richard pressed his lips together in thought. "Could we look for more now?" he asked, already on his feet and moving toward the bookshelves. "Just for a little while?" he pleaded. He sounded like a little boy and managed to look like one, too, opening his eyes wide and pouting. I got to my feet, smoothing the wrinkles from my skirt and tucking my hair behind my ears. "Okay," I said. "You asked for it."

I didn't mind at all having him help me sort. It was like having an assistant on the job. Soon I'd pretty well forgotten we were looking for household records and had lapsed into my real job of cataloging. We managed to accomplish quite a bit, from my viewpoint — and nothing at all, from Richard's — over the next several hours. No more account books came to light.

Richard was at one end of a row of bookshelves and I at the other, planning to meet in the middle. Before we got there, he called me over.

"Look at this!" He held out what appeared from a distance to be a piece of cardboard not much bigger than an index card.

When I got closer, I saw it was a picture. Creased in several places, it was beginning to yellow with age. It showed two tiny children, all bundled up in snowsuits, only their eyes peeking out at the camera. They sat on a sled. It was one of those old-fashioned kind with curved, metal runners. In the background was the house on Echo Moon.

"Huh," I pondered, taking the photo out of his hand and turning it over. On the back, all it said was: *Winter, 1957*. There were no names, no ages.

"I wonder who they are," I said, handing it back. "Where did you find it?"

"It fell out of this book." He showed me the volume. A cookbook the size of a Bible. One of those soup-to-nuts kinds with lots of oddly colored photographs of crown roasts and Christmas cookies. My mother had one just like it. Come to think of it, so did I. It seemed a bit strange to me that Roland Clayton had one.

Richard's words echoed my thoughts. "Clayton really did collect everything, didn't he?" He flipped through the pages, looking at the women in frilly aprons, proudly displaying the finished products. Shaking his head, he said, "Are there other cookbooks in here? This doesn't seem to mesh with the other stuff we've gone through. Histories, literature, biographies, art books."

It was the first one I'd seen, but then there was a lot still unsorted. Maybe I hadn't reached that section yet. The proverbial light bulb went on.

"I'll check the inventory." I hurried over to the desk where the ledger sat in plain sight. "When I looked earlier, it seemed to be arranged alphabetically, by the title. This title shouldn't be hard to find." Seating myself in the big wooden chair, I took the ledger off the pile. Then I stopped dead. Lying there peacefully, gleaming in the light from the desk lamp, was the key to the library.

My forehead furrowed as I looked at it, waiting for an explanation to materialize. None did.

"Here's the key!" I held it up for Richard to see. "On the desk. But I know I took it with me."

Richard joined me and perched on the corner of the desk, the cookbook still in his hand. "Well, you know what my mother always said. 'It didn't get up and walk away by itself.' You must have forgotten it here." He sounded calm and composed. As if it didn't matter.

I opened my mouth to start defending myself again, but it seemed pointless. "Maybe I did," I said, and maybe I really had.

I leafed through the inventory looking for *The Hungry Hubby Cookbook*, but it wasn't listed. "I don't see it," I said, "but then my track record's not very good today. You look." I thrust the book into his hands and waited while he double-checked. I turned the library key over and over in my hand, puzzled, and finally shrugged it off. I had been in a hurry when I left.

"Nope, it's not in here," Richard pronounced, closing the book with a *thwap*. "Unless it's out of order." He cupped his chin in his palm and rested his elbow on one knee.

"Possible but unlikely," I said.

"Maybe," he mused, "it's someone else's book."

Suddenly this seemed obvious. And the obvious owner was —

"Janet Peabody!" we said at the same time, smiling at each other triumphantly.

"And if it isn't hers, she's still the only logical person who might know its owner."

"Then, by extension, she would know who is in the picture too. There must be photo albums in the house." Richard shook the photo in the air. "This belongs with the others."

"In the archives?" I teased, but he didn't smile.

"Yes," he said, climbing onto what I soon realized was a soapbox.

For the next five minutes he presented me with a well-prepared lecture, complete with emphatic hand gestures, on the historical importance of good recordkeeping and note taking, explaining the twofold function of such.

"It provides a living record of the times, in general," he said, ticking it off on his index finger. "It also leaves an accurate family record for all genealogical purposes, making tracing a family tree much simpler. When I think of all the research time that could be saved if only people had taken a moment to jot down details!"

Obviously this was a subject dear to his heart. Being an antiques appraiser, the connection was readily apparent. To authenticate an antique took time, research, and accuracy.

"You're right," I jumped in when he paused to take a breath. "Why don't I ask Janet about the book and the picture next time she's free? She'll be able to set us straight." I rose from my chair as I spoke, taking the book inventory and the cookbook with its precious photo inside in one hand. The pesky library key I grasped firmly in the other. Arching my stiff back, I stifled a yawn. As we'd worked, the hour had grown late, and now I was exhausted.

"I've had enough for one day," I said. "You too?"

Richard stood by the window, looking out at the garden. Now he nodded slowly, pushing one hand through his thick dark hair. "Me too," he agreed.

I joined him at the window, and it felt quite natural when he slipped his arm around my shoulders.

We stood silently a moment. The gardens outside were bathed in silver from the moon overhead. No breeze came tonight, so the scene was still. I sighed quite happily and relaxed in Richard's arms.

Then, out in the garden, near the far hedge, I saw a flash of light. Immediately remembering last night's light in the woods, I pointed. "Did you see that?"

Richard looked in the direction I indicated. "See what?"

"A light. I saw a light, there. Who is it, do you think?" I spoke in a whisper, even though we stood in a lighted room and were surely visible to anyone outside.

"There! There it is again!"

Richard's grip on my shoulders tightened. "You must be tired." He gave a chuckle. "That was a firefly. There's another, and another, and another." He started to laugh in earnest as the light show went on, and I gave him a good-natured poke in the ribs.

I pulled the curtains shut and flicked off the desk lamp. Richard watched me lock the door that night and saw me carry the key into my room. I crawled into bed in a dreamy mood. He'd kissed me good night at my door.

Chapter Six

The next day I was up with the birds. I'd slept soundly, with no chair beneath the doorknob. As I dressed for work in pink twill trousers and a matching checkered blouse, I even hummed a bit of a tune. It was a glorious day, I had my job to look forward to, and maybe — just maybe — I'd met someone special.

I took a little extra time with my makeup that morning, adding eye shadow and mascara to my usual blush-and-lipstick routine. I clipped my hair back with a big pink bow, feeling frivolous and pretty.

On the way out the door, I remembered the cookbook with the photo inside and retrieved it from the bottom dresser drawer, where I had placed it for safekeeping the night before. Tucking it under my arm, I snatched the library key and pushed it deep into my pocket, then headed off in search of breakfast.

The day before, we had eaten in the dining room, English style, with hot plates on the sideboard. Today I was too early for that and made directly for the big kitchen Janet had shown me when I'd first arrived. I pushed open the swinging wooden door and entered her domain.

This was definitely a cook's kitchen, with plenty of countertop working space and a wall full of cupboards. Blue-and-white delftlike tiles covered the lower two thirds of the other walls; copper pots and pans hung above. There was a modern refrigerator in one corner, but the stove dated from the forties. Standing at it now, with her back to me, was Janet Peabody. Her feet in their sensible shoes were planted firmly apart as she struggled to stir a big batch of what smelled like oatmeal. As I approached, she added a touch of milk to make the chore easier.

"Good morning, Janet. That smells good!"

She turned to look at me over her shoulder. "Oh, good morning, Sarah. You're up early."

I nodded, feeling ebullient, and impulsively gave her a quick hug. "Who could sleep on such a beautiful day?"

Her hand paused in its circular path, and she gave me an appraising look. At that moment she seemed old and wise. I knew she could read my mind. "It seems to me something other than oatmeal is cooking," she declared.

I couldn't help myself and laughed out loud. "You could be right!" I said. "But it's too soon to tell."

Her eyes disappeared into creases and wrinkles when she smiled. She squeezed my hand. "Well, I can't say I'm surprised. The minute I saw you, I said to myself, 'Now here's a girl for Andrew.' He's a splendid man. Quite a catch."

My smile didn't falter as she extolled the virtues of our boss. I wasn't sure how to correct her. The last thing I wanted to do was burst her bubble, but I also couldn't let her think I was scheming to "catch" Andrew Clayton.

Finally I said simply, "Time will tell." She winked at me then, and I felt like a traitor.

When I glanced nervously away, I saw the cookbook, lying where I had left it on the battered old table in the middle of the room. It was just the change of subject I needed.

"Janet," I began as I picked it up and brought it to the stove, "I found this in the library last night, and I'm not sure it belongs there. Is it yours, by any chance?"

She turned off the heat under the bubbling pot, wiping her hands on the red apron she wore. When she saw the book I held, the curiosity vanished from her face, to be replaced by what could only be fear. Her eyes grew wide; her mouth opened and closed as if she couldn't find any words. Her usually rosy cheeks paled in an instant. With surprising strength she wrenched the book from my hands.

"Where did you find it?" she whispered rapidly, clutching it against her chest. "Where?"

Puzzled, I hurried to explain. "Richard found it. On a bookshelf. It seemed out of place."

She nodded, gray hair bobbing once, twice. She walked away from me, across the room, and I followed in confusion.

"There's a picture inside," I offered, pointing at the book. "Richard thought you might know who is in it. He thinks it should be with the other family photographs. If it's even family." I shrugged.

Janet didn't really seem to be listening to me and said, "Yes, yes," in a distracted tone. Then she stooped to open the cupboard directly in front of us. I had a quick view of soup cans and cake mixes as she thrust the book haphazardly inside, closing the door with a bang.

When she straightened up, the mood had passed. The roses were back in her cheeks, and only her rapid breathing gave away her anxiety. "Would you like a cup of coffee, Sarah?" she asked, glancing at me without meeting my eyes.

"Um, sure." It was apparent we were not going to discuss the book or the photograph. I had no idea why; neither one seemed very important. Certainly I hadn't expected such a dramatic reaction.

Janet hadn't struck me as particularly quirky, but now I had reason to wonder what all the years of island isolation had done to her. The question just flitted through my mind and was rapidly dismissed. Another odd event.

As I took the cup of steaming coffee she set on the table before me, helping myself to marmalade and toast, it dawned on me that plenty of odd things had happened over the last several days. But then, I mused, I'd taken this job as a kind of adventure, and that's exactly what I'd gotten. New experiences, new surroundings, new people. A vision of the Old Curiosity Shop popped into my head. The sturdy wooden bookcases dating from the 1920's, the old brass cash register I refused to part with even though it was occasionally stubborn, and the big bow window in the front of the store combined to give the dear little place quite an atmosphere. I loved its warmth, its personality. It made a cozy haven from the rest of the world, just as the island provided a haven for Janet. It was wonderful to have a place so special, removed from the wider community of the world. But was it good to live there all the time? Would it be better to be more in touch and less protected? In forty years, would I be like Janet and Frank, secretive and eccentric?

Echo Moon Island was an unusual place. In less than three days it had me questioning the focal point of my life — the bookstore.

"Must be the lake air," I said to myself. Janet was across the room at the stove again, scrambling a mountain of eggs, and didn't hear me.

A moment later the kitchen door swung open and Richard appeared. He wore a pair of dark-blue coveralls, looking more like one of his workmen than their boss. One lock of dark hair jutted up, as if he'd slept on it wrong. It made him look younger than his years, and I smiled.

"Morning, ladies!" he called cheerily, making a beeline for the coffeepot.

Janet hurried to fill a platter with eggs and handed it to him as he went by. "Good morning, Richard." Her eyes darted to the clock. "You're right on schedule."

As I watched in amused silence, she led the procession from the kitchen to the dining room, carrying the toast rack and the bacon on a tray. Richard brought up the rear with the eggs and coffeepot.

"Come join me," he suggested as he passed. Happily I picked up my plate and rose to follow. "Don't forget the marmalade!" he said over his shoulder, and I went back to retrieve it.

After we had set the items down on the sideboard, Richard placed a gentle hand on Janet's shoulder, stopping her in her retreat to the kitchen. He looked from me to her as he spoke. "Sarah and I were wondering —" he began. I immediately knew what his next words would be and shook my head to ward off the question. Janet couldn't see me, but Richard did and smoothly finished the sentence, "what time lunch is today."

Janet frowned. "Twelve noon, same as always."

"Ah, as I thought," Richard said. "Thank you."

When Janet left the room and we were alone, he asked, "What gives?"

Heaving a sigh, I pulled out one of the heavy dining-room chairs and sat down, hooking my feet on the elaborately carved crossbar at the bottom. While he filled a plate with a sampling of everything, I told him of Janet's reaction to the book.

"Honestly, Richard, I thought she was going to faint. She turned white as a sheet. Then she just shoved the book into a cupboard, as if she couldn't stand the sight of it. She was afraid! Afraid of a book!" I propped both elbows on the table and leaned closer. "Who would be afraid of a book? Especially a cookbook. That's crazy!"

He shook his head, chewed, swallowed. Reaching for a big glass of orange juice, he said, "It does seem funny, you're right." He sipped the fresh-squeezed fruit juice and thought for a moment. A light came into his eyes, mischievous and amused. Dropping his voice low, he said, "Do you think it's . . . mysterious?" Giving an exaggerated shudder of terror, he grinned. "It seems to me you have a vivid imagination, Sarah. Ghosts, fireflies, lost keys. Now this. Are you easily excitable?" He calmly buttered another slice of toast, not glancing up to see my reaction. I knew he was just baiting me and tried to keep my temper. "Do you read a lot of mysteries in your bookstore?"

Pressing my lips together, I counted rapidly to ten. He didn't know about Frank's warning, I reminded myself. He didn't know about the note in my room. If I was excitable, I thought I had reason to be.

His cavalier attitude stopped me from confiding these other events. Once again I was reminded that I really didn't know very much about him. As much as I recoiled from the idea, I couldn't deny the possibility that he had left the note. Although he would have no reason that I was aware of, he could have done it. Frank could have done it. Andrew could have done it, for that matter. But who would play tricks on a stranger?

"You're probably right. It's all in my head," I said for his benefit, taking the toast he held out to me. I lifted my shoulders in a shrug. "It must be this place. So old, so lonely." Looking around the dining room, with its dark wood and crystal, I realized that my description was accurate. It was definitely old; that point couldn't be argued. But it also seemed lonely. Empty of emotion or atmosphere, it was as if no one lived here at all. Frank and Janet must normally live in silence, I thought, picturing the house without the workmen, without Richard and me. When Andrew was in town during the week, the place would be positively dreary.

That imagination of mine conjured up a winter scene. Snowbound, with the lake frozen over and the north wind battering against the windows, Echo Moon would be a haven to no one. Tingles raced up my arms as the vision took hold and I shivered.

"Cold?"

Richard's voice pushed the picture away, and I blinked with surprise.

"No, no." I poured more coffee into our cups and glanced at my watch. It was still early, but I had plenty to accomplish today. Pushing back my chair, I said, "May as well get to work. I'll see you at lunch."

Richard smiled, producing a warm glow deep inside me. I smiled back.

The library waited quietly and, after unlocking the door, my first action was to go to the windows and open the curtains. Sunlight already filled the garden, and I decided to ask Andrew if I could borrow one of the bicycles for a ride after work. There was plenty of island left to explore, and today would be a good day to start.

Resolutely turning my back on the view, I settled in to work, pulling my supplies from the desk drawer. I worked straight through without stopping, doing paperwork for an hour and then manual labor — carrying, stacking, and sorting — for the next. By lunchtime I was ready for a break.

Standing in the middle of the room, seeing order starting to take place, I felt a great thrill. It was quite a challenge, getting this huge collection into shape, but I found I was genuinely enjoying it. The Claytons had plenty of treasures in the library, and it was a pleasure to handle them. Some of the books were worthless, of course, and I had a separate area of the room set aside for the books I would recommend discarding. But there were many books which my university-trained eye recognized as rare. First editions, classics in mint condition, unbroken complete works that had managed to avoid being damaged over the years. They might not compare to Shakespeare's folios, but they were still valuable and could fetch quite a price on the open market.

Idly, I wondered if the house was adequately insured. Of course, I reasoned, Roland Clayton had probably had the collection appraised at the time of his self-styled inventory. I made a mental note to check with Andrew the next time I saw him.

As it turned out, I got my opportunity just moments later. We met in the hall. He had just come in from the conservatory, and his hands were covered in dark, rich soil from the plants. The knees of his pants were scuffed.

"I've been puttering," he confessed, holding his hands together to keep the dirt from falling onto Janet's clean floor. "Frank hates it when I do that, but I enjoy a little contact with nature now and then."

"I'd think there was enough garden to go around," I said, thinking of the huge area outside the library. "The grounds here. . . ." I let the sentence trail off as Andrew nodded.

"Yes," he said abruptly. "Sometimes Frank forgets who is master of Echo Moon. He needs to be reminded every so often." His eyes lost their calm blue intensity for an instant, and something else took its place. They had a hard, brittle look I knew instantly I would never want to have aimed at me.

"I'm just on the way to lunch," I said, switching topics. "I'll see you there?"

"As soon as I wash this off." He indicated his hands. "I'll be along in a few minutes."

When he turned toward the stairs, I continued to the dining room.

It was probably a good thing he and Frank saw each other only on weekends, I decided. Apparently they just couldn't get along. Andrew did seem to be a bit overbearing and, for an instant, sympathy for Frank welled within me. It couldn't have been easy to see a young man take over responsibilities that had once been his.

Janet had explained at tea that first day

how Andrew had come to the island, living with his uncle after his parents' deaths. Ironically, they'd been killed in a train wreck. Little Andrew had arrived on Echo Moon shortly after his first birthday. It was no wonder he viewed Janet as a mother. She'd been the only one he'd ever really known.

I walked into the dining room, filled with pity for both men. The little boy without parents and the older man unappreciated and disliked by the boy he'd watched grow up.

My own childhood had been peaceful and without turmoil. No tragedies marred my memories. We didn't have the Clayton money, but we had something much more precious. We had love.

Wistful and nostalgic, I sat down at the table in what was becoming my chair. Andrew's place was at the head of table, by the fireplace. I sat on his left in the chair nearest him, and Richard was next to me. Chuck and Joe sat opposite us. So far all of us had not been at the table at the same time, but if we were, the seating arrangements were already determined.

Now, just Chuck and Joe shared the room with me, and we exchanged greetings. For them, this consisted of glancing up from their overburdened plates, bobbing their heads as they chewed, and looking back down at their next forkful.

Naturally I'd been hoping Richard would be there. I was anxious to show him a book I'd found in my morning's labors. It was titled *Historical Homes of the Midwest*. It was a slim volume, more like a pamphlet than a book, actually. Grainy photographs of the estates of land barons, captains of industry, and politicians spilled over its pages. There was no mention of the Claytons anywhere, which seemed rather funny to me. But it was a small publication, put out by a local historical society, so it couldn't be considered comprehensive. Still, I thought Richard might like to see it. Maybe there was a useful detail for his research buried within.

As I nibbled from a plateful of fruit salad, I turned the pages of the book. It wasn't old, compared to some others in the library, and had been produced in the 1960's, according to the title page.

"Hmm," I murmured, spooning up another tangy bit of orange. Not for the life of me would I tell Richard I thought it was strange that a local publication totally ignored an area landmark, as I assumed Echo Moon would be. He'd just make a ghoulish face and accuse me of wild interpretation.

Still, I was entitled to my opinion, and that was it.

All three of us looked up as Andrew appeared, clean and tidy. He took his place with a smile, his eyes moving to each of us in turn.

I was relieved when he began to question Chuck about the progress in the music room, forcing the workman to give more than one-word answers and drawing him out. Their conversation made it possible for me to continue leafing through the book, hoping I'd spy something spectacular.

After about five minutes both the pamphlet and Chuck had said all they had to say. I pushed the book aside just as Andrew turned to me.

"Oh!" I said, remembering the question I'd wanted to ask. My request for a bicycle was readily granted. He even gave me a suggested route to follow, through the south end of the island.

"The northern portion of the island is a little more rugged," he explained. "The southern area is every bit as beautiful, but the shoreline isn't as rocky." He helped himself to salad, replacing the serving dish after offering me some. "And there are no hills," he added. His voice was serious, but his eyes weren't, and I knew he was recalling my last gasping strokes up the hill the day before.

"That's good news," I admitted. My legs ached slightly from the unexpected strain, and I had no desire to make them any worse.

I was about to ask my insurance question then, but decided against it at the last minute. I wouldn't want him to think I was poking my nose into business that wasn't any of mine. *When we talk about the library, I thought, it'll seem natural to bring it up. I'll just wait until then.*

Would anything have turned out differently if I'd asked that day?

Chapter Seven

During the next week or so, my life on the island developed a routine. After work each day I'd walk over to the aging brick barn where the horses, carriages, and bicycles were kept. I collected the bike I'd thought of as mine since I'd used it for my tour of the island with Andrew, and set off on one of the island's trails. It was an exhilarating feeling, to be out in the fresh air and sunshine after looking at it from inside the library all day.

My work in the library was important and interesting, but too sedentary to suit me. Stretching my legs by circling the island made me feel wonderful. It cleared the book dust from my brain and improved my perspective.

My trips were always solo ones, which was exactly what I wanted. I couldn't explain to Richard that I needed time by myself without making him think I was avoiding him, so I slipped out without telling anyone the first few times. Soon the pattern was established and Richard would say,

"When you're back from your ride, let me know."

I really wasn't trying to keep my distance. He and I spent most evenings together, doing recreational reading or watching the ancient television. The TV was tucked into a room off the main hallway that must have served as a study when Roland was alive. The furniture was battered and worn and had obviously been moved here out of sight because of its run-down condition. That just made it more cozy, reminding me of the old days with my parents. Then, as now, I'd tucked my feet up beneath me and lost myself in a book. Here on the island it was Richard sharing the sofa instead of Mom or Dad.

It was all very peaceful and domestic. There were no further notes in my room or warnings from Frank. I carried the key to the library on a chain around my neck, and if lights bobbed in the woods, they did it when I wasn't looking. I never forgot the incidents, though, and, being an orderly sort by nature, filed them away in my memory bank.

One evening Richard and I sat in companionable silence, engrossed in our various books. He was earning his keep, leafing through antique reference books, trying to trace that elusive wallpaper order he'd found earlier. I must confess, I had succumbed to the lure of fiction and was rapidly falling under the spell of Wilkie Collins and his gothic tales of ethereal white visions on dark country roads. The edition was from the Clayton library, of course, but wasn't a first edition. If it hadn't been dog-eared, I would never have borrowed it.

Sitting in a plaid wing chair across the room, Richard looked over at me as I sat with the book, turning pages with my right hand and munching grapes from a bowl with my left. He said, "You know, I must tell you, I've never really understood why Andrew hired you." At my startled look he went on. "Here he brings in you — someone from far away — and pays you a pretty penny, I'm sure, to do a job that I could have done just as well."

He shook his head, unable to fathom the depths of our employer's mind. For a moment I just stared at him, puzzled. Was he jealous? Did he think I was overpaid? Compared to whom? Him?

Reluctantly I closed Mr. Collins and spoke. "You know about rare-book collections?"

Richard's eyebrows raised, as if in disbelief. "Well, I am in antiques," he said in a patronizing tone. "A related area, I'd say."

I swung my feet out from beneath me to the floor. I was barefoot. My sandals lay haphazardly on the rug, and now I worked my toes into them. "Related, perhaps. But with a collection as valuable as this one, a specialist was definitely in order, you must admit."

Richard shrugged. "I just think I could have handled it. My shop has an area devoted to books. I've dealt with rare books in the past. Appraising, finding buyers, wheeling and dealing to get the best price. It was just a surprise to me that Andrew hired another person for the job."

"Well, he can certainly afford it," I pointed out, my voice rising in volume. "And he wants the work completed as soon as possible. If you were doing both jobs, it would take twice as long."

Turning back to the book spread out before him, Richard gave another nonchalant shrug. "That may be true, Sarah. I'd never presume to know Andrew's motives." He looked down at the page, dismissing the topic, and I wanted to grab him by the shoulders and give him a shake.

Instead, I crossed the room and stood in front of the lamp next to his chair.

"You're blocking the light, Sarah. Could you please move?"

Childishly I stood my ground. "Don't you think I'm capable of this job, Richard? Are you questioning my ability? Why? What have I done wrong?" I knew I was following correct procedures. I knew my job was professional and thorough. I wanted to know why Richard suddenly thought it was lacking, why he thought he could do it better.

"I don't think you fully understand my job here, Richard," I continued, feeling angry at his casual dismissal. "I'm not just determining which books are worth money and which are not. I'm not merely appraising. I'll be cataloging them as well. Organizing them by Dewey-decimal numbers, turning a book collection into a library!" By the end of my speech, I was practically yelling, and I was sending thundering looks at him. He, in turn, had ceased to look at his book and watched me, openmouthed.

When I finished, there was silence. I clasped my hands in front of me, looking at my toes, wondering fleetingly if I'd overreacted. My blood pounded in my ears with my heartbeat. I worked hard at my job. I was a professional every bit as much as Richard. It was unfair of him to dismiss my work and claim he could do it without the proper training. Unfair, and unlike him. At least, it was unlike the man I'd known thus far.

Now he rose from his chair slowly, and his hands grasped my elbows, pulling me into the circle of his arms. "I meant no offense, Sarah." He tipped my chin up, making me look into his eyes. "Please accept my apology. My last intention was to slight your ability." He smiled, and I noticed the creases at the corners of his eyes, the one deep line across his forehead. Up close like this, I could see green specks in the brown depths of his eyes. Colors from nature, comforting and tranquil. I had to say it.

"Apology accepted."

Just as my heartbeat was returning to normal, he kissed me and sent it soaring once more. Closing my eyes, I relaxed against him, enjoying the feel of his lips on mine, his arms holding me close. Richard ended the embrace by giving me a bear hug, affectionate and a little overwhelming.

Not content to leave well enough alone, I asked him, "What prompted all that? Why are you questioning my position here?"

His arms fell away, and he heaved a sigh. Running a hand through his hair, he said, "Andrew came to me today, complaining about how long the work was taking. He asked me for a projected completion date, and when I told him the music room wouldn't be finished for at least two weeks, he nearly exploded."

I remembered that nasty glint I'd seen in Andrew's eyes when he spoke of Frank Peabody, and I could imagine how he must have looked truly angry. It was a frightening thought.

"Why?" I asked.

Richard made a face. "He started ranting about money. Said he wasn't a billionaire and couldn't afford to keep paying all these people indefinitely." He gave a snort of sarcastic laughter. "All four of us."

"Hmm." I pondered, confused. "But he told me this work was funded by money left in Roland's will. It isn't really costing Andrew a cent."

Again Richard shrugged, shaking his head. "Makes you feel positively unwelcome, doesn't it?"

"Not only that, Richard. It just seems as though Andrew would want to make his uncle's last wish come true. It's his job, of course, as executor of the estate, but you'd think he'd want to do it, anyway." I frowned. "Just out of love, you know?"

"Far be it from me to second-guess our boss," he said, reaching for me once more.

"Better add this to your list of odd events."

"Maybe I will. And in the meantime I'll try to move a little faster on the job. I'd hate to be terminated and have to leave the library unfinished."

"Your dedication is admirable," he told me, his lips just brushing my cheek. "I only hope it's not misplaced." He stopped my next question before I could phrase it, pressing his lips to mine and driving out coherent thought.

It was several moments before I was aware of my surroundings again. When Richard gently pushed back the bangs drooping over my forehead, his tenderness stirred me. I hadn't meant this to happen. My goal had been adventure, not romance.

But I wasn't about to argue with fate.

Two days later I was hard at work, seated at the desk with the propped-up leg, when the library door opened and Andrew appeared. He was wearing a lightweight gray suit and looked as good as I'd thought he would.

"Hello," I said, smiling broadly but inwardly churning. Was it my turn to be asked for a deadline? My turn to be told, "Speed it up"?

He returned my smile and crossed the

room. "How is it going, Sarah? Having any luck?" He glanced down at the work cards scattered across the surface of the desk.

"Oh, yes. I've begun cataloging. As I proceed, I'll be cleaning the books and, as an extra measure, checking the titles against the '86 inventory. It's all coming together quite nicely."

"That's welcome news. I must admit, the place certainly looks better." He swiveled his gaze around the library. Books were no longer stacked on the floor or piled sideways on the shelves. It was beginning to look less like an explosion in a publisher's warehouse and more like the Old Curiosity Shop. Andrew approved. I could tell by the way he bobbed his head and murmured, "Mmhmm, mmhmm."

Silently I let out the breath I'd been anxiously holding.

He turned back to me. "I'm going to be gone a few days. Business in town. Janet has the phone number where I can be reached, if you need it."

"Oh, thank you for telling me. I'll remember that." I gave him a nod, expecting him to leave then. But he didn't. He lingered on, wandering around the room wordlessly and eventually returning to my desk.

Standing at my elbow, looking over my

shoulder at the opened volumes of classification catalogs, he said, "This is a lot more complicated than I thought it would be. I had no idea how involved it is."

To me, of course, it didn't seem complicated. It seemed precise. But to someone unfamiliar with the process, it probably came as a surprise.

"Good cataloging takes time," I admitted. "But it's the only kind worth having."

"Oh, yes, I'm sure," Andrew hastened to agree, straightening up and turning away. His hand went to his tie, tightening the knot at his throat. He spun back around. "You will be finished by the end of the summer, though, won't you?" His eyes had narrowed, and just a slash of their bright blue shone out at me. His words hadn't been demanding or accusing, just curious.

I reassured him. "Oh, yes. In fact, if I continue at my present rate of production, I could be done by early August." When he nodded, appearing relieved, I felt it was safe to ask. "Is there any problem, Andrew? Do you need the work done sooner? I could work longer hours, if you want."

I made the offer genuinely. After over two weeks on the job, I'd gotten a bit possessive with the collection. I wanted the best for it and wouldn't let a little thing like not receiving extra money for the extra work stop me. I was being paid a salary, not an hourly wage, so actually, the sooner the work was done, the better it would be for me, from a financial standpoint. Now that my heart had entangled itself with Richard's, though, practical considerations didn't matter. I refused to think about the future off the island, about what would happen to me — to us — when our jobs were done.

"Oh, I don't think that will be necessary, Sarah," he said, wandering across the room to where the shelves of "discard" books were kept. His eyes raced over the spines, reading titles. "All these are to be sold?" he asked.

I nodded. "Sold or just plain discarded. They're of little value. Either damaged beyond repair or common, readily available titles. I'd advise selling what you can and donating the rest to charity."

When he turned again to look at me, there was a spark in his eye. "Sell them to a dealer, you mean? Like you, perhaps?"

I shrugged and said casually, "Perhaps. Some of the titles would do well in my store, but I'm in no position to offer you a price for all of them."

He pulled a saggy old copy of *Tom Sawyer* off the shelf. The illustrations were nice, but the spine was cracked, the end papers were torn, and at some point it had been stored near dampness. Little specks of mold dotted the cover.

"Your references for this job were impeccable, Sarah. I know you would never even consider slipping one of Uncle's treasures into the pile of rubbish, then buying it for your own shop later." He riffled the pages of the book, sending its musty odor into the air. "I do know that, don't I?"

His tone challenged me, and I knew in an instant what he was really saying. He was implying I was capable of stealing. I could barely believe my ears and felt my face grow hot with indignation.

Shaking inside, I pushed back my chair and rose, straightening up to my full height, rigid with anger. When I spoke, my tone was cold. "Are you suggesting I'm a thief? That I'm just waiting for an opportunity to pilfer your property and make a tidy profit on the side? I don't know what makes you ask me such a question, but I can assure you I am honest and above reproach. If you checked my references, you should know that. If you can doubt my motivation and my ability to perform this job, then perhaps I should just leave now and you can allow someone else to finish the work!" My voice had miraculously remained even and controlled. Although my anger burned, I felt detached from my body and was able to deliver my response with my wits about me.

Andrew began to chuckle, tossing back his head and giving great unmusical hoots of laughter. I backed a step or two closer to the door, wondering at his crazy mood shifts, his intense emotional array. It was very bewildering and not a little frightening.

"Sarah, Sarah," he said, setting old Tom back on the shelf and walking toward me slowly, still smiling in amusement. "Don't misunderstand. I wasn't accusing you of any wrongdoing. I was just thinking out loud. Being in charge of all this valuable property is a big job. I must protect it at all costs." He held out his arms, embracing his estate.

"Protect it from whom?" My words were brittle, icy with the anger coursing through me. I crossed my arms over my chest and waited for an answer. *Andrew Clayton holds little charm now*, I thought, wondering what Janet would think.

He frowned, looking confused and befuddled. At last he answered softly, "You never know." Putting his hand to his forehead, he gave me a kind of salute and stalked across the room to the door. With his hand on the knob, he called back to me, "Keep up the good work."

The glass in the doors rattled after he'd shut them. I heard his steps fading away down the corridor and took a deep breath.

He had seemed so friendly when we first met. Now, as the anger drained away, I wondered who was the real Andrew — the congenial businessman wreathed in smiles or the flinty, accusing rich man, certain he was being bilked by his employees.

I ran my hands up over my arms, trying to bring them back to life. The little episode had totally broken my concentration, and I looked absently at the work spread across my desk.

"Where was I when I was so rudely interrupted?" I asked aloud. There was no one to answer me, so I sorted it out on my own, forcing my thoughts back to books and away from the unsettling topic of my employer. By the time Janet came to announce dinner was ready, I'd pushed the incident back into that growing file in my memory labeled "Odd Events."

Richard refilled my coffee cup and handed around the plate of cookies Janet had made for dessert that night. "I'm going ashore tomorrow, Sarah. Some business in town. Would you like to come with me?" His invitation was informal and welcome.

As soon as I finished swallowing, I answered, "I'd love to!"

My enthusiasm made him smile, and he gave my hand a squeeze. "Good. We'll leave just after breakfast and be back before dark."

I nodded. "It sounds wonderful." All I could think of was how good it would be to spend some time off the island. Spending it with Richard would be a bonus. "How will we get to shore?" I asked practically. "Do you have a boat?"

He wrinkled his nose in distaste. "Just barely," he admitted. "It's an old rowboat with a cranky outboard motor. Not much to look at, not too fast, and not very comfortable, either."

"I'm glad it's only a five-mile trip," I laughed. "You make it sound just lovely."

"Well, I want you to be prepared."

"After the *Molly Jane*, how bad could it be?"

We set a time to meet the next morning and tucked into the last of the cookies.

That night, I sat up in bed reading my gothic novel. I knew it wasn't a terrific idea and was bound to induce the jitters, but I was nearing the end and anxious to read the outcome. In books all the scary things are explained away and reasons are given for Odd Events and surprising behavior.

It would certainly be nice to have some reasons here, I thought, closing the book with a sigh. But real life isn't like fiction, and I would have to wait quite a while for my answers.

Chapter Eight

The noise of the outboard motor made normal conversation all but impossible. Aside from a few shouted remarks to each other, Richard and I were silent on the trip to the mainland. I didn't mind, because it gave me a chance to appreciate the beauty of our surroundings.

The sun glinted off the waves, and I had to squint against its glare. Taking deep breaths of the fresh, clean air, I felt the peaceful atmosphere invading my body. The sense of calm was accented by the cries of the gulls overhead, and I leaned back to watch them wheel and dive above me. Reluctantly I realized we were nearing the shore. When Richard cut the engine, my ears rang with the sudden silence.

We docked at the same pier where the *Molly Jane* sat, pulling the little rowboat's nose up onto shore and securing the line. Next to the tug, it looked especially tiny and fragile, making me glad we had another day of clear skies and sunshine. I wouldn't want to cross the lake during a storm. There were plenty of shipwreck stories in the area, some dating back hundreds of years. I had no desire to become part of a new one.

Richard took my hand as we walked to the Clayton storehouse, where his car was parked alongside mine. It was wonderful to hold his hand, warm and firm, swinging gently at my side. The prospect of an entire day together made my heart soar.

Janet hadn't looked too pleased at the breakfast table when she'd heard our plan. Her eyes clouded over, and a stern, disapproving scowl marred her apple-pie countenance. "On business, is it?" she'd questioned Richard sharply.

He'd glanced from her to me, and I was careful to keep my expression blank, although I wanted to laugh at the comic image she presented, bread knife in one hand, toast rack in the other.

"Yes, of course," Richard said. "Clayton business, actually. We won't be long, but don't wait dinner for us." He gave a charming smile, and I watched in amazement as Janet dimpled as well.

"That's fine, then," she declared. "Have a pleasant outing." Her customary humming began as she left the room.

Now, as Richard held open the car door and I climbed into the station wagon, I put all thoughts of Janet and her plans for my love life on the back burner. She belonged to the island, and today did not.

Richard started the engine and put the car in gear, leaving the storehouse behind and turning onto the narrow blacktop road leading to town.

"First off," he began, plotting an itinerary, "I'd like to stop off at a friend's in Rifkin. Emil Fincher owns an antique store there. Specializes in Victoriana. I'm hoping he can give me a lead with the Clayton place."

As we drove, he'd occasionally take his eyes off the road to look over at me. Making sure I was awake, I think, because the hour was still quite early. He needn't have feared. I was keeping busy looking around me at the charming old homes lining the street. When I'd passed through this town on my way here, I'd had to focus all my attention on the road, making sure I didn't miss the turnoff and get lost. I hadn't had a chance to appreciate the quaint gingerbread structures, looking for all the world like an ad for Smalltown, USA. Soon, though, the houses were farther apart; then rolling fields of corn began to separate farms and the town was left behind.

I turned away from the pastoral scene and

asked Richard's profile, "How far is it to Rifkin?"

He glanced over at me, lips pressed together in thought. "About fifty miles," he said at last, accelerating into the passing lane to overtake a lumbering tractor. "We should be there in an hour or so." I still must have looked sleepy because he added thoughtfully, "Go ahead and nap, if you like. I'll wake you when we get there."

"No, no." I stifled a yawn with the back of my hand. "I'm awake now. That fresh air on the water did it."

Richard laughed, unconvinced. "Whatever you say." He reached over and switched on the car radio, filling the interior with soft music.

The road stretched out before us, black and winding, and I leaned back against the seat, settling in for the ride, relaxed and eager. On my lap I held the library inventory. Richard had suggested I bring along something to read, and I chose this. Not exactly riveting, I suppose, but I'd finished Wilkie Collins and welcomed a chance to delve further into Roland Clayton's well-structured document.

Inside of five minutes I'd lost track of my surroundings, reading each entry carefully, bringing a mental picture of the book to mind. According to Roland's notes, many of the volumes had been gifts from family and friends who knew of his collection. Many others had been purchased through a book dealer in Milwaukee. His name was listed near the front of the inventory. It was one I recognized. For these entries, Roland had included the price he'd paid for each book and its appraised value at the time of the inventory.

The appraised amounts were always hundreds and hundreds of dollars, as would be expected. I hefted the heavy ledger in both hands, thinking of how many books there were and guessing at their total value, and I let out a low whistle, wondering again about adequate insurance. Many of the volumes were irreplaceable. I fished in my purse for a notebook and pen, making a note to ask Andrew at the earliest convenience.

We traveled on, slowing as we passed through tiny towns, speeding up again at their outskirts. Richard hummed along with the radio, and I joined him for a lighthearted duet on some of the more familiar numbers.

"Interesting reading?" he asked after our moving rendition of "We Are the World."

I held up the ledger for him to see. "I'm on the job and hard at work," I claimed with a laugh. Sobering, I went on to relate Andrew's inquiry into the length of my project and the horrid, uncalled-for remarks which had followed. "Do you honestly think he believes I'd steal?" I asked, still aghast at the accusation.

"If he doubted your honesty or your motives, he wouldn't have hired you, I'm sure," he said, and I wished I could believe him.

"But then why even make the suggestion?" I closed the book and turned as much as my seat belt would allow to face Richard. He glanced over, then returned his eyes to the road.

"Hey, don't look at me for an answer there. I've been accused of padding the payroll by dragging out the work time. I'd like a few answers myself."

I heaved a sigh. "I never expected this when I agreed to come here."

Richard smiled in sympathy. He reached over to take my hand and give it a squeeze. "Don't worry about it, Sarah. Andrew is a rich young man, well on his way to eccentricity, judging by recent behavior. It has nothing to do with you or me or the way we do our jobs."

This time I knew he was right and felt better just by being reassured. "You know," I said playfully, "Janet thinks I'd make the perfect Mrs. Clayton." I watched his face carefully as I said the words and was rewarded by the deep frown that instantly appeared.

"Oh, really?" His words were tight, and I knew he was trying not to seem interested.

"Yes," I said, still holding his hand, running my fingers over the fine dark hairs that covered its surface. "She said the minute she saw me, she knew I was just the girl for Andrew."

"Well, now, that's a problem." Richard's voice dropped, low and soft. I held my breath, inching closer on my seat, the safety belt tugging against my chest as I waited for his next words. "The minute I saw you," he said at last, eyes steady on the road, "I knew you were just the girl for me." He darted a glance at me, and I saw him smile, his brown eyes sparkling intently.

My own response came from deep within, filling me with pleasure and finally exploding into a grin that stretched the figurative ear to ear. Straining my seat belt as far as it would go, I leaned over to kiss his smooth, clean-shaven cheek. He smelled clean and warm, with no after-shave overpowering his own special scent. My lips danced a path from cheekbone to chin, ending with a resounding smack.

"Whoa, there!" he called out, his hand resting against my cheek. "None of that in the car. Sit still!"

Obediently I returned to my seat, still smiling. "You win," I said, and we both knew exactly what I meant.

Richard stopped the car as a big wagon piled high with hay pulled out from a side street, crossing our path before heading in the opposite direction. He took the opportunity to lean toward me. I met him halfway, and our lips did the rest.

When we arrived in Ritkin, a cherry-red sign proclaimed *Welcome*, and we were immediately plunged into the shopping district. Little storefronts lined either side of the street. The brick buildings were obviously old but had undergone recent face-lifts and were now charming Victorian images. Bay windows enabled the merchants to display their wares to best advantage, while white bric-a-brac edged the doorways. On the sidewalks tall wrought-iron lampposts stood sentinel, their frosted-glass globes adding to the gaslit impression.

My head swiveled from side to side, and I took a deep breath.

Richard took the words out of my mouth by saying in a high-pitched squeal meant to be a female voice, "It's so cute!"

I whirled around to look at him and was surprised to see a comic smirk on his handsome face.

"That is what you were going to say, right?" he asked, and I nodded mutely. "Well, don't," he suggested. "It's just too cute for words."

"You don't like it?" I couldn't believe he didn't find the updated antique street adorable. "It's so old-fashioned," I pointed out, jabbing a finger at the candy-striped barber pole outside one store. "Old-fashioned is your business."

"Yes, but this is newfangled old-fashioned. Gingerbread run amuck for the sake of tourism. It isn't real. It's too sweet. Too perfect."

Silently I considered his remarks. We were pulling up outside a two-story cream-brick building with FINCHER ANTIQUES stenciled in gold across the front windows. "Only to a purist like you," I decided at last. "I still like it."

"Hmph!" Richard shut off the engine. As he slammed shut the car door and led the way to the store, he reminded me, "You're a tourist, after all."

I could hardly deny that, but it didn't prevent me from sweeping past him into the store. Was there no romance in his soul? Why couldn't something be sweet and perfect? Unbidden, an image of my father scoffing at my mother's dusty collection of porcelain dolls came to mind. The tiny dolls were charming, delightful to look at, fragile to touch.

"Clutter!" Dad had declared.

Maybe all men were the same, I generalized, blinking as my eyes adjusted to the dim interior of the shop. I held out my hand, and Richard caught it in his.

The store was small and crowded. Narrow and long, it had an unpolished wood floor that creaked beneath our feet. The walls were lined with shelves filled to overflowing. There didn't appear to be any particular order to the display. Children's toys shared space with ancient kitchen utensils. Rocking chairs and rocking horses took up floor space in one corner. Near the back of the shop, a little nook caught my eye, and I recognized the ever-familiar shape of books, books, books. Drawn like a magnet, I tugged on Richard's arm.

"Let's go over there. By the books."

Richard resisted my efforts to pull him in that direction. "You go ahead. I'm going to find Emil."

While I headed eagerly for the bookshelves, he walked over to the glass display case in the middle of the store, where jewelry glistened inside and an adding machine sat on top. His hand darted out to give the little silver bell sitting there a sharp tap. Its tinny sound filled the shop and, far away, I heard footsteps slowly shuffle closer. The floorboards just beyond the book nook gave a protesting groan, and I looked up from my perusal of dusty titles.

Emil — for surely this wizened old gent had to be the man in question — was a small, thin man, looking as fragile as some of his antiques. Sparse gray hair grew in a tuft circling his head. Little gold-framed glasses perched on the very edge of his nose, and even though the day was warm, he wore a red cardigan sweater over a sports shirt and baggy, faded jeans. He didn't lift his gaze from his shoes as he went by and managed to move much more rapidly than I would have expected.

I heard him greet Richard with an enthusiastic shout and smiled as I pictured them clapping each other on the back. Turning back to the bookcase, I continued to scan the spines, keeping my hands at my sides and resisting the urge to examine each book. I was truly on a busman's holiday.

It was several moments later when a title

leaped out at me from one of the higher shelves. So familiar, but from where? I wondered as I stretched up as high as I could. A few well-placed pokes from underneath, and the book slipped easily into my hands.

A Historian's History of Western Civilization.

I ran my finger over the weathered brown cover. All the gilt of the lettering had worn away, and it was just a trick of the light that enabled me to make out the title at all.

As I stood, rooted in place, I realized my hands were shaking, as if they already knew what I was about to discover. A burst of laughter from the front of the store startled me, and I jumped. Just Richard and Emil sharing an "old" joke, I thought, mildly amused at the pun. Then once more I turned my attention to the book in my hands. Holding my breath, I opened the cover.

Inscribed inside were the words: *To Rollie, with affection. From Viola.*

Rollie. Roland? Viola. The old girl?

Chapter Nine

The words swam before my eyes, fading on the page and then jumping out at me once more. Richard and Emil continued their conversation at the entrance. The soft drone of their voices just reached me. I was glad for a few moments alone to ponder and assess.

Could this be a book from the library on Echo Moon Island? If so, how had it found its way into this shop? Who had taken it from the untidy library and brought it here?

One question tumbled rapidly onto another, faster than I could sort out possible answers. All I knew for certain was I had never seen this book before, but I had read Roland Clayton's description of it in the inventory. In 1986 it had been part of the collection. According to the inventory, it still was. There were no notations saying the volume had been discarded. I remembered it so well because of the lighthearted remark in the margin of its entry: *Gift from the old girl*. Andrew had interrupted me that morning in the library, caught me daydreaming over who "the old girl" could be. Now, I was certain I had part of the answer. Her name was Viola. And I held her gift in my hands.

Before I could draw any further conclusions or even do any mad speculation, Richard and Emil came wandering toward me. Whatever their business had been, it must have proven successful because they both looked quite pleased with themselves.

Richard put an arm around the older gent's shoulders, towering over him like a benevolent giant. "Sarah, I'd like you to meet Emil Fincher. Great friend of mine and the best in the business." His eyes moved from one of us to the other.

I shifted the book to my left hand and shook the aged, wrinkled hand extended to me. "It's a pleasure to meet you, Mr. Fincher. You've got a wonderful store here. I could browse for hours!"

Mr. Fincher's watery blue eyes looked into mine, and I knew instantly that despite his feeble appearance, not much got past him. "I see you've already found a treasure, hmm?" He indicated the book.

Maybe more than you realize, I thought. But I just smiled and said, "You're right. I simply must have it. Name your price." I held the book out and watched Richard's face for possible reaction. It showed nothing but mild curiosity. Some of the dark foreboding that had settled near my heart lifted. I didn't want to think any disloyal thoughts, but some disturbing facts couldn't be denied, and they brought up plenty of questions. Questions I'd rather not have the answers to just then.

"For a friend of Richard's it must be a gift." Emil's words broke into my gloomy train of thought. He placed the book gently back into my hands, giving me a tight-lipped smile. "Please accept it as a souvenir of your first visit to my shop."

"Thank you. I will."

"Sarah owns a bookstore, you know," Richard put in, sounding rather proud.

Emil asked me a few questions about the store, and our conversation turned into a business discussion. If there is one thing I love as much as books, it's talking about books. In no time at all I'd forgotten the mystery attached to my new possession and was deep in a debate on the best way to market rare volumes.

"Why don't we continue this over coffee?" Emil suggested, ambling off toward the front of the store.

Richard and I trailed behind, and I saw Richard glance swiftly at his wristwatch.

"Sure, we've got time," he said, looking to me for agreement.

"We've got all day, remember?"

Emil locked up the shop, and we crossed the road in a charming red-brick crosswalk to a little restaurant called, not surprisingly, Mom's Diner. Once inside, we waited for a gingham-clad waitress to show us to a table. The place was filled with the buzz of conversation, and from our spot near the rear, I was able to take a good look at our surroundings.

None of the eight or nine tables matched, I noticed in amusement. All were heavy, wooden, farmhouse-kitchen tables with wide, comfortable chairs. Some were round, while others — like ours — were square. Green plants hung from every available space, blending well with the wood carvings and cross-stitch samplers used as wall decorations. Our coffee came in blue-and-white speckled mugs, while cream poured from a container shaped like a cow. Everything was neat and tidy, enhanced by the country music playing in the background.

Richard must hate it, I thought wryly and tried to catch his eye. The breakfast menu came between us, however, and I had to content myself with gently nudging his foot under the table.

After we had placed our order, I turned to Emil. "I'll bet you come here every day for lunch."

He sipped his coffee slowly, noisily. The cup and saucer clinked together. Then he said, "Just about. It's a tourist trap, of course. But the food is good."

It was Richard's turn to catch my eye. He leaned back in his chair and crossed his arms over his chest, smiling triumphantly. "Sarah thinks it's charming. Don't you, Sarah?"

I'm afraid my answering grin gave me away. "Well, yes, I do," I admitted.

Nodding, Emil pushed his glasses up his nose and settled his elbows on the tabletop. "Then our money was well spent. I'm a member of the Chamber of Commerce here, and it was our goal to be what tourists would expect a small town to be. Quaint. Rustic."

Richard scowled in disapproval. "What for?"

"What for?" Emil quoted back, spreading his arms wide to indicate the busy diner, filled with local folk and tourists alike. The bell above the doorjangled as more customers entered. "Look around you, man! Rifkin's in the black now. We're turning a profit, and that's good news for everyone. Why, someday we'll be as popular as all those Door County towns." He brought his fist down on the tabletop just hard enough to make the unmatched silverware dance.

All Wisconsin residents knew Door County and its jaunty, nautical towns with names like Egg Harbor and Fish Creek. The summer combination of blue skies and sparkling waters made them irresistible. Rifkin was nowhere near the lake, of course, but it was on the way to the Door, and I could easily see it as a stop for northern-bound vacationers.

During the pause in conversation as the waitress brought our orders, I reached a conclusion. "Richard, you're too much of a historian to appreciate this face-lift. But even you must admit it indicates not all progress is bad." I picked up my knife and liberally spread a slice of homemade raisin bread with red raspberry jam.

"I'm not against progress or profit," Richard defended himself. "Within reason."

"And we've gone too far?" Emil's voice dared him to answer.

I took a big bite and chewed complacently, wondering how Richard would answer honestly and not anger his friend.

"Let's just say you've come awfully close," Richard returned, reaching for the pepper shaker and attacking his eggs with it. "Better stop now before the water turns to soda pop and sugarplums grow on the trees." His voice had a bluntly sarcastic tone, and I shifted uncomfortably, swallowing my food and leaping into the conversation.

"Now, now. This is no time for architectural debate. If you don't like Rifkin, don't visit. Or visit with your eyes closed. Whatever you think, Richard, it's too late to do anything about it now."

Emil caught my eye and nodded. "Richard and I have never seen eye to eye on some things," he admitted, talking about the man as if he were in the next room and not three feet across the table. "He's headstrong, you know." Emil wagged a finger at me, shaking his head and causing his glasses to slip down his nose. "Be warned, Sarah, Richard is an opinionated man. He doesn't easily take no for an answer." He turned, looking steadily at Richard before adding, "Or take well-meant advice from his friends."

The atmosphere at our table in the cheerful, friendly diner was suddenly tense and oppressive. Apparently these two had secrets. Recent or long past, I couldn't tell. But whatever these secrets were, it was easy to see Richard intended for them to remain buried away.

Looking over his shoulder, he signaled the waitress for more coffee. When he turned back to us, the annoyed look I'd seen cross his face was gone. Brows no longer knit but raised in anticipation, he gave a broad smile and rubbed his hands together.

"Let's talk about something else," he suggested.

I, for one, was glad to comply. While my conscious mind had been listening to the Rifkin Rebeautification Debate, my subconscious had been formulating questions for Emil Fincher. Who better than the owner to explain where his merchandise came from?

"I'm interested in where you find all your marvelous things," I said, sincere and curious. "Do you go to estate sales, or do people come to you?"

Spooning sugar into his coffee, Emil replied, "Well, both, of course. Like Richard, I look for good stock — valuable items in decent condition that I can get at a good price. And, well" — that tight-lipped smile flashed again — "I'm a reputable dealer, so people come to me." He wasn't bragging — or suffering from false modesty. Clearly he enjoyed his work and was good at it.

"Give me an example," I said, leading him in the direction I wanted. "Like, oh, how about my book?" I realized my ploy wasn't very subtle, but curiosity got the best of me. Verbal fencing has never been my strong point, and in this instance my straightforward question got me nowhere.

"Oh, I really couldn't say off the top of my head," Emil explained with a chuckle. "I do have a lively business during these summer months, and things change hands rapidly."

My hopeful expression crumbled, and I tried gamely to hide my disappointment. With a shrug, I said, "It really doesn't matter."

"I could check, if you'd like," Emil offered, and the temptation to learn the truth proved too great. This time, though, I hid my enthusiasm behind a smile and said oh-so-casually, "Only if it isn't any bother. I'd like to see if whoever it was has some other titles I've been searching for."

Emil gave a nod of understanding, his fringe of hair bobbing in agreement. "For a customer or your own collection?"

"Both. I'm my own best customer," I confessed, and my two companions joined in my laughter. I guess I wasn't the only dealer who snapped up the items that caught his or her eye before anyone else got a chance to see them.

Emil pushed his plate toward the center of the table, reaching for his wallet and making general time-to-go motions. "This has been very enjoyable," he said, getting to his feet and beaming his slender smile at each of us in turn. "But it's time for me to get back to business. Not all of us have the luxury of free time." He surprised me then by giving a teasing wink over Richard's shoulder.

Richard gave a good-natured snort and remarked, "No, just the four months you spend in Arizona every winter."

"Well, aside from that. . . ." Emil let the sentence trail off while Richard shook his head. "Good luck with your work. Hope you find what you need to finish it up." Turning to me, he said, "And, Sarah, where can I contact you with the information on that book?"

"I should be on the island through August, at the rate I'm going. A letter there should reach me."

"Consider it done." With one last wave, he ambled off to the cashier, and we could hear him carrying on a conversation with the fresh-faced hostess running the register. Soon her tinkle of laughter came and Richard said, "He's amazing. Seventy years old and he's still got a way with women."

I drained the last of the coffee from my cup, then dabbed at my lips with a blue cloth napkin. "He's a nice man," I agreed. "Will he be able to help you with your research?" I pushed back my chair.

"I should think so. If he hasn't already given me the right source" — he patted his shirt pocket, and I heard the crinkle of paper — "he'll keep digging till he finds it."

"Lucky for you," I said, following him as he led the way to the front of the diner. After he had paid the bill, we walked to the car and within minutes were back on the highway, Rifkin fading rapidly in the rear-view mirror.

While Richard concentrated on the driving, I paged carefully through my new book, looking for anything that could serve as further evidence that the book had once belonged to Roland Clayton.

"Maybe he'll turn up a dealer's name for you too," Richard commented, noticing my preoccupation.

Sunshine streamed in the windows, warming my face with its glow. White, fluffy summertime clouds hung in the brightest blue sky. If I were on vacation, this would be a perfect day. But I was working — on a puzzle. *I hope he doesn't give me your name,* I thought. Aloud I said, "Maybe," and continued to flick the pages.

Richard was silent nearly the entire ride into South Clifton, where his business was based. I spent the time sorting through the facts as I knew them, trying to find a different interpretation.

But I couldn't.

With a furrowed brow I ran through them once more. One: Richard had been on the island for at least two weeks before my arrival. At that time the library had been a mess. No one would ever notice a book or two missing. He had had the opportunity. Two: He had told me in no uncertain terms that he'd dealt with old books before. That he knew where and how to get the best prices. Even today he'd confessed he had nothing against making a profit. So there was a motive — the oldest one around.

Looking at his rugged profile, returning his smile when he caught me staring, I couldn't believe Richard could be involved in what amounted to book theft. Emil Fincher didn't strike me as the kind of man who would knowingly deal in stolen goods, either. I doubted he'd aid and abet, even for a friend. And if Richard were guilty, would he have mentioned his own knowledge of books, giving me just enough information to be curious? Wouldn't he have covered up that knowledge, so when the missing volumes were discovered, his name wouldn't immediately pop to mind?

With a sigh I closed the book and, leaning forward, set it carefully on the floor between my feet. Taking sunglasses from my purse and putting them on, I said, "I think I'll take that nap now."

"All right. I'll wake you." Richard's eyes never left the road, and I closed mine, leaning my head back against the seat.

In the old days the Indians of Guatemala had a custom using six tiny dolls. "Trouble dolls," they were called. At night you took one doll for each of your worries and told it the problem. Then you placed the doll under your pillow. At night, while you slept, the doll would solve your problem, and when you woke in the morning, you'd have the answer. Just before I slipped off in a doze, I wondered where I could get my hands on some of those dolls when Guatemala was so far away.

Chapter Ten

Richard's hand gently shook my shoulder, and my eyelids opened and closed a few times. For a moment I had that confused and embarrassed feeling you get waking up in a strange place, not knowing exactly where you are, feeling exposed somehow. But then I focused and saw him unlatching his seat belt and removing the keys from the ignition.

Straightening in my seat, I gave a contented yawn. That nap had done the trick, all right. I felt rested and ready to carry on, asking questions and facing the truth. Whatever it was.

"You snore. Did you know that?" Richard's voice held a hint of amusement and surprise as he looked at me in something resembling astonishment. One corner of his mouth curved up in a teasing grin, and he shook his head in disbelief. "You looked so beautiful, fast asleep. All innocent and angelic," he continued in a singsong tone. "Till the sawing started!" He wrinkled his nose and accompanied the action by doing an impression of someone — presumably me — snoring.

My sleep-contented smile vanished in an instant and, in mock anger, I gave him a swat on the arm. "How dare you?" I demanded loftily, putting my nose in the air. "I don't believe you, and even if it were true, you couldn't prove it."

"It's true. Trust me."

"Hmph!" I scrambled to follow him as he opened the car door and stepped out. Only then did I stop to look around me. We were parked outside an old brick building set in the middle of a large, gravel-filled lot. There weren't many other buildings nearby. In fact, the closest was a good block and a half off and had a parking lot full of what appeared to be rusty car parts. Judging from the dreary condition of that structure and the isolated location of this, I figured we were in an industrial area of some sort.

"Where are we?" I asked as Richard inserted a key into the sturdy lock on the door of the building and, with the help of a well-aimed shoulder, pushed it open.

The door gave a protesting groan of metal hinges. Together we stepped into a dark and musty room, several degrees cooler than the day outside. I clasped Richard's arm and repeated my question.

His hand found the light switch, and the room flooded with fluorescent glow. "My warehouse," he said simply.

With the lights on, the antiques dealer's stock was revealed. Or, at least, hinted at. Dust cloths made huge, lumpy statues of the furniture beneath them. Wooden packing crates lined the walls, reducing the floor surface of the building and making it seem much smaller than it had appeared from outside.

"Oh," I said, leaving his side to wander around the room, lifting the corners of the cloths and peering beneath them. "This is your shop?" I asked, dusting off my dirty hands on one of the cloths and making a face. "It's awfully messy. How do you find anything?" Gingerly I tested an old rocking chair, hoping it would hold my weight. It did.

Richard moved around the room methodically, swerving around the crates on the floor, making his way to an area near the back where a desk with a telephone comprised an office. "First off, this isn't my shop. It's my warehouse. The shop is in town, operated daily by my dear Aunt Lydia while I'm away. It's clean and tidy and perfectly presentable, I assure you. Secondly, this place is messy because I haven't been here much lately. But even if I were, it would be easy to find anything I might be looking for, because I'm organized." By the time he said this, he was opening and closing the desk drawers rapid-fire.

"Oh, really?"

"Yes, really!" With a muttered curse, he flopped down in the chair behind the desk and began rummaging through mountains of papers, examining each one before tossing it aside onto another heap.

Crossing the room, I stood at his shoulder, out of range of the flying papers. I reached out and placed my hand on top of his thick, soft hair, stroking it as if it were a cat. The bright light overhead made it shine, almost sparkling where the first few silver hairs had crept in. "Do you need help?" I asked and found myself petting the air as Richard knelt down to open the desk's bottom drawer, removing himself from my reach.

"Uh-no, no," he said, coming up with a handful of manila folders. "Just looking for a reference. . . ." His voice trailed off as he concentrated on the sheet before him. With one finger he traced the surface of each page, his eyes scanning it rapidly.

I tilted my head, my hair falling over one shoulder, and tried to read the pages with him, but I couldn't make out the words. It looked like a lot of unorganized notes. Nothing coherent or orderly that I could see.

In no time I lost interest in Richard's search and resumed poking around the warehouse, peeking into boxes and resisting the urge to touch the delicate items I discovered. When I slid back the cover of one box, however, I couldn't stifle my cry of delight.

Inside, on a bed of straw, lay a porcelain doll, much like the kind my mother had collected. This one was only six inches tall, dressed as a southern belle in blue-and-white gown, complete with lace-edged petticoats. The lace had grown tattered and dingy with time, and some of the paint had chipped off her curls, but she was lovely.

Carefully, so carefully, I lifted her out. Cradling her in both hands, I brought her closer for a better look. Lips still red, eyes black, her expression was not the blank one of some dolls, but a cheerful and excited one. As if, I thought, she'd just caught a glimpse of someone special and was holding back a smile. I traced the outline of her lips, where the faintest curve upward melted into a rosy cheek, and found myself smiling in response.

When Richard spoke from directly behind

me, I started in surprise and tightened my grip on the tiny figure.

"What have you found?" he asked, putting his arm around my shoulder.

Wordlessly I opened my hands to reveal the doll. "Oh, yes. It's a good one, isn't it?" he said. "But I have some better ones. Over here, I think." He took a few steps away from me, in the direction of another crate.

"No, don't," I told him. "I don't want to see any others. I like this one. May I buy her, please?"

"But that's not a very special one, Sarah," Richard said, delving into the box closest at hand. "It's not very valuable. Just an ordinary child's toy. Let me find you a gem." He spoke with his back to me, head down and rummaging, reminding me of a dog digging for a bone.

"I don't want a gem." I tugged on his shirttail. "Richard, stop. I've found this one, and I want this one. How much?"

Turning, he straightened and grinned at me in the bright light. For a moment we just looked at each other. "Did she say, 'Take me home'?" he asked then, in a tone that made it clear he'd heard the same voice. Our eyes met, and I felt a glow of satisfaction.

"As a matter of fact, yes."

"Well, then, by all means." He gave a courtly bow and covered my hands with his own. "She is yours." He brought my hands to his lips and pressed a kiss against them.

"Thank you." The words came out as a whisper. I took a step toward him, drawn by the warmth of his hand around mine, and our lips met over entwined fingers. Tender yet firm, Richard's kiss sent me tingling. Still holding the doll, I slid my arms around his neck, willing the kiss to go on. Even after our lips parted, we stood together, cuddled close for several long, enjoyable moments.

Richard pulled away from me, lifting his chin from where it had rested on the top of my head. Looking down at me, he said, "Well, we could stand here all day like this, and it would suit me just fine." He glanced over his shoulder to the door. "But I know the sun is shining outside on a gorgeous day, and I don't think we should spend it indoors."

I nodded in agreement, waiting to see what his next suggestion would be, since it was obvious he had something in mind.

"What would you say to a picnic? We could pick up some food here in town, then find a nice patch of quiet shoreline on the way back to the island."

I could already feel the sun beaming down on us and hear the water splashing over the rocky shore. "Sounds perfect! Let's go!"

We stopped just long enough to place the doll back in her straw-lined bed for traveling, then went in search of a convenience store for our impromptu picnic fare. Sandwiches, chips, fruit, soda, and giant chocolate-chip cookies sat invitingly in a bag on the backseat as we headed for an area of state park not far off.

The station wagon moved slowly over the narrow gravel road leading deep into a wooded area, curving sharply around a huge stand of pine trees which blocked out the sun. We parked alongside several other cars, but there were no fellow picnickers in sight. Richard said the spot was popular with hikers and bikers, pointing at the elaborate bike rack on one car's roof. "Must be off on the trails."

Glancing at the smooth trail I saw heading off into the woods, I sighed, wishing we had bicycles along. The day was just right for a long trek — sunny, but with just enough clouds to keep down the glare and virtually no wind to pedal against.

I took Richard's hand as he led the way to the bluff that overlooked Lake Michigan. "Next time we'll bring bikes!" I told him.

He dropped a light kiss onto my forehead without breaking stride. " 'Next time.' I like the sound of that."

I had to admit, so did I.

Richard spread the battered blue blanket he'd found in the car over the smooth green grass on the cliff's edge. Before us stretched the lake, a deeper blue than the sky today, patterned with waves. I looked north to where the coast jutted out. The roots of trees growing on the hillside poked through the bluff into the air and dangled precariously, victims of erosion. One old birch had been bent by the wind until it was nearly even with the earth.

At our backs, the woods rose, high and majestic. A breath of breeze moved through the treetops, singing softly and bringing with it the scent of the pines. Feeling lazy and contented, I flopped down unceremoniously, stretching my legs out and leaning back on my elbows.

"You know, before I came here, I'd only seen this lake once," I said wistfully. "And now I can't imagine being away from it."

Richard rummaged in the grocery sack, pulling out each item and laying it next to him on the cloth. My remark didn't disrupt his actions, although he gave a grunt of acknowledgement. Intent on assembling lunch, his hands moved rapidly, distributing our feast. "It's been known to have that effect," he remarked, tucking the empty grocery sack under a corner of the blanket. I popped open my soda can and took a sip, then turned my attention to the sandwich.

As we ate, Richard began to talk of his work on the island, and I figured the time I'd spent napping in the car he had used for planning. Now he was planning aloud. He explained the steps they'd be taking to return the mosaic floor of the music room to its former glory before moving on to the ladies' parlor downstairs.

"Luckily the work needed there isn't nearly as extensive. Pretty straightforward, actually."

Reaching for the bag of potato chips, I asked, "What about the wallpaper? When will you be able to finish that up?"

For a moment his brow wrinkled, and I knew he wasn't sure what I was talking about. Then his expression cleared, and he said in an offhand way, "Oh, that's all taken care of. We'll hang the stuff this week."

I crunched a chip, wondering if I'd heard wrong. "But did you find the same design as the original? Wouldn't something like that have to be specially made?"

Richard sighed and peeled a banana. "Yes, an old design could be reproduced just for us. And I thought that was Clayton's idea. However, I have since been told otherwise."

This was news to me, and I was burning with curiosity. "What happened?"

He shrugged. "I explained the situation to Clayton. Told him there was a good chance I could find a record of the original and have some reproduced. He didn't want to wait that long. 'Time is money,' he said. Can you believe it?" He shook his head, then bit off the tip of the banana.

"At this point, I'd believe anything. He seems to be changing his tune quite regularly." I thought again of his verbal assault on me, questioning my honesty. What would he think, I wondered, if he saw my new book — the one I was sure belonged on Echo Moon? I shifted uncomfortably, not liking the directions my thoughts were taking.

"So I brought him a catalog of readily available reproductions, and he picked one out. We ordered the paper last week. It should arrive with the supplies day after tomorrow." He sounded resigned and disappointed, cheated of the chance to do a genuine recreation. The integrity of his work meant a lot to him, I knew, and I could understand his desire to do the best possible job. I was the same way.

"No one will be able to tell," I said, trying to placate him.

"That's true. And it isn't my house, so I'll do as I'm told."

He passed me an orange, and I peeled it thoughtfully. "Wait a minute. I thought we came to town so you could check with Mr. Fincher about tracing the pattern."

Richard looked up rapidly, then his eyes darted away. "Yeah, well. . . ." He stalled for time, and all my suspicions came flooding back tenfold. Had he met with Emil about getting more books from the library to sell?

"Why did we come, Richard?" I pressed him. My fingers dug nervously into the flesh of the orange, spilling sweet, sticky juice onto my hands. Across from me on the blanket, he drew his knees up, resting his folded arms on them.

"Because I need his help," he said. "There's something I can't quite figure out, and I'm hoping he can. Do I have to be specific?" He held out his hand, and I put a segment of orange into it. For a moment we were quiet, eating the fruit in a heavy silence.

"Yes, please," I urged. "Be specific."

"Okay, but I've warned you. I don't understand it."

I smiled, although I didn't feel very happy. "Maybe if you tell me, we can figure it out together."

"Fair enough." He turned away to pick up the bag containing dessert. Handing me one of the giant chocolate-chip cookies, he began, "You remember how I told you I'd found a record of Roland Clayton's paintings? A book similar to the library inventory. A necessity for insurance purposes, I'd assume, and handy for me." He broke his own cookie into several pieces and ate one rapidly. "It lists the contents of each room — what paintings hung where, the artist's name, where and when each painting was obtained. It's very complete, and that's what is causing the problem."

I nodded, looking down at the cookie I held, absently counting the number of visible chips.

"If it were a sporadic record, I could assume things had been left out. Misplaced. But it isn't, so I can't."

"What?"

"It's so detailed. I'm convinced if something is missing, it shouldn't be."

My heart began to beat faster, and I drew

in a shallow breath. I looked up. "And is something missing?"

Our eyes met. Richard looked genuinely puzzled, his eyes cloudy with doubt, expression open and guileless. "Yes," he said a little too loudly. "Several minor works listed in the record book as belonging in the music room seem to have vanished."

"Were they around when you started on that room?"

He popped another bit of cookie into his mouth, eyes trained off over the lake, thoughtful. "No," he said at last, shaking his head. "Clayton told me he had had Peabody remove the paintings and bric-a-brac. Said they were to be stored in the attic so there would be no risk of damage. I didn't think anything of it at the time. It just saved us some work. Those things would have to be moved before we could begin."

He polished off the last of the cookie, brushing his hands free of crumbs and reaching for a napkin. "I never checked to see if what he said was true. I had no reason to doubt his word, after all."

"But now you do?"

He paused, pressing his lips into a thin, grim line. "Yes, I do. The paintings that were supposedly removed and stored by Frank Peabody are not where I was told they would be. I looked for them in the attic yesterday and couldn't locate them."

"Maybe you looked in the wrong part of the attic," I suggested, envisioning the cavernous region the attic must be. "Did you have Peabody — er, Frank — show you where he put them?"

"When they weren't where I expected to find them, I searched for that cranky old devil for an hour. Seemed he'd been misplaced too." He laughed and I had to join in.

Frank did give every appearance of being out of place. I'd seen him from the library windows, riding the lawn mower or wandering the grounds with a shovel in one hand and gardening tools in the other. He always wore the same expression: None. It was as if he were a robot, going through the motions of living without really taking part. Even when he'd been on the receiving end of Andrew's anger that very first day on the dock, he'd looked bored.

"Did he ever turn up?"

Richard started stowing the remains of the picnic into the grocery sack from whence they came. Over one shoulder he said, "Oh, yes. Hours later. When I questioned him after dinner, he gave me some vague directions no one could interpret." Here he flapped his hands, pointing in two directions at the same time in imitation of Frank. "I'm sure he thought I'd just drop it, but I didn't. I made him show me where he'd put them. Marched him right up there and said, 'Point!' "

"And?" I prodded.

"And he pointed into a dark, dusty corner where there were no paintings and no footprints in the dust. They'd never been there, and he knew it." Richard's voice was animated and full of frustration. He crumpled up the grocery bag in one angry motion.

"Then what?"

He lifted his shoulders. "We went back downstairs."

"Back downstairs?" I echoed.

He nodded. "What else could I do? It was clear he had no answers." Wrinkling his brows, he added, "Although whether or not he could have answered, I don't know. I just don't trust that man."

I had no illusions about Frank Peabody, either. My minimal contact had been enough for me to know not to look to him for help or sympathy. "So what are you saying? You think Frank swiped the paintings?" I tried to keep the amazement from my voice, but the idea of poky old Frank spiriting away priceless artwork made me want to laugh. "I can't believe that, Richard.

What does he know about art?"

Richard shifted on the blanket. "You don't have to be an expert to realize they're valuable. You don't need to be an art historian to figure that out."

"Yes, but why would he do it? What would he need money for?"

Shrugging, Richard said, "Who can tell? He seems an odd duck. Hard to predict the behavior of an odd duck."

He came to sit beside me in the space where the food had been spread, slipping his arm easily around my shoulders. I leaned up against the breadth of his chest, closing my eyes and letting the sun bathe me in its warmth.

Suddenly there were no mysteries, and my interest in our conversation evaporated like a raindrop in July. "Who cares about old Frank Peabody?" I murmured, and Richard dropped a gentle kiss on my temple.

"It'll sort itself out, I suppose." His lips were at my ear, my cheek, my mouth.

The troubles of the world fell away as we kissed, and there was only this place and this man. For several long moments we were alone in the universe of our own creation. I thought my brain had shut down entirely and was rather surprised when something went "click."

With effort I pulled away from my place in his arms, just far enough so I could look at him. "What does Emil Fincher have to do with the missing paintings?"

Richard laughed, gathering me close for one of his enthusiastic bear hugs. "You're like a terrier with a bone," he teased. "I went to Emil because he has connections in the field." He gave me a knowing look. "Good and bad."

My mouth dropped open. "Bad? Outside the law? Illegal? Not on the up-and-up?"

Richard rolled his eyes skyward. "Yes. He doesn't deal with them; he just knows them," he clarified. "Emil is as honest as they come."

My imagination took off, and I tried out the most recent pieces to the puzzle, all thoughts of romance gone. "You went to see Emil so you could ask him about the paintings. See if he'd heard of any of them being available recently. On the black market, so to speak." I tapped my jawbone with my index finger and plotted. "Now, he's given you a list of less-than-reputable dealers to consult, in a casual way, while you play detective."

Richard clapped his hands slowly. "Very good, Sherlock. Go to the head of the class."

My triumph at the cleverness of my deduction was short-lived. "Couldn't that be a little dangerous? You shouldn't poke your nose in with criminals. You could get hurt."

"So instead I should just let Peabody cart away the rest of the collection and wait for Clayton to notice? He'd end up blaming me."

"Hmm." My finger resumed its tapping. Richard had accused me of seeing monsters where there were none. Now it was my turn. "It seems to me you're skipping a few steps, Richard, and jumping to conclusions. First off, maybe Frank just forgot where he put the pictures. He's a little forgetful, so that's possible. Second, you haven't got one stitch of proof it's Frank stealing the stuff, if it is stolen." I cast about for another suspect. "Maybe it's Janet. Or your workmen. Or the ghost of Echo Moon. Thirdly, the logical next step is to go to Andrew and let him deal with it. It's his property and his problem. You weren't hired to be a private investigator, after all." I'd ticked off the points on my fingers and now held them up for Richard to see. "That's what I'd do. Go to Andrew."

Thinking about my own problem, I wondered if I should follow my own advice and consult the boss. Almost before I had the thought, I dismissed it. I wouldn't mention the traveling book to anyone until I had done a little checking on my own. Do as I say, not as I do, I thought with a wry smile.

To his credit, Richard had listened to me without interrupting. Now he nodded. "I'll admit, it may look like I've created a conspiracy theory, but I've just got a feeling. Something's definitely wrong." He shrugged. "Maybe I should go to Clayton and dump it in his lap. He could have moved the pictures himself, I suppose."

"Well, there's one way to find out." I smiled. "When Andrew gets back from his trip, just ask him. He'll probably be able to clear this up in no time, and you won't have to go skulking around in the Art Underworld." I gave the words capital letters, dropping my voice low and mysterious.

"I really don't think this will end up so tidy, Sarah. But I promise I won't go charging into a thieves' den without trying every other avenue first."

"Or without inviting me along," I added with a grin.

We rose to our feet, and I arched my stiff back. Together we folded the blanket, tossed the garbage into a big wire bin near the parking lot, and returned to the car. In no time we'd left the quiet of the forest and were humming along the highway. Soon we'd be back on the island, with all its puzzles.

I reached over and covered Richard's hand on the steering wheel with my own. He took his eyes off the road just long enough to give me a smile.

Richard couldn't be guilty of any crime, my heart told me. But the book on the floor between my feet said, *Don't be too sure.*

I was starting to get a headache.

Chapter Eleven

The next day, after lunch, Richard hurried back to work while I lingered over iced tea. My work was progressing at a suitable pace. I'd been using the inventory extensively, checking off each entry after it had been located, catalogued, and cleaned. There were a few titles listed I hadn't run across yet, but I was holding out hope that they'd still surface. Lazily I got to my feet, gathering up the dirty dishes and carrying them into the kitchen.

Janet looked up as I entered. Her eyebrows shot up under her fringe of gray hair, and her lips pursed into a sharp O. "Sarah, you don't have to do the cleaning up! You've got your own work to do." She made shooing motions with her hands as I turned away from the sink.

"Don't scold me, Janet. I want to help." With a sheepish grin I confessed my feelings. "I don't feel like working just now. I think I need a break."

The creases in her cheeks deepened as she grinned. "Well, in that case, let's get started."

Together we made short work of the dishes. Janet chattered away as she vigorously scrubbed at plates and glasses. I added my two cents to the conversation as I dried and stacked the clean utensils. Her stories of the old days on Echo Moon were fascinating, and we stayed talking long after the chores were complete.

Janet led the way out the back door and eased herself onto the porch step. I joined her, feeling only slightly guilty about enjoying the sunny day. Her eyes swept over the backyard, taking in amazingly well-ordered rose beds and gently swaying maple trees reaching skyward.

"I remember when those trees were planted," she said, her voice taking on that rosy-hued tone we all get when speaking of the past. "Frank worked all afternoon digging the holes just where Mr. Roland wanted them. And the boys wanted to help, of course." She made a noise curiously like a giggle, looking at the base of the biggest tree. From her misty eyes and tender smile, I could tell she was seeing that long-ago scene.

"What boys?" I asked, following her gaze and squinting, as if, with a little effort, I could see them too.

"Andrew and Johnny," she said without

hesitation. "Oh, what a pair they were!" She laughed out loud, clapping her hands together in her lap. "Always into things, of course. Such natural curiosity. Wasn't easy to keep up with those two. What one wasn't doing, the other was." A faint smile tipped up the corners of her mouth. Her eyes remained unfocused on some vision of her own.

As she spoke, I remembered the picture of two bundled-up children we'd found in the cookbook and Janet's odd reaction to it. Andrew and Johnny?

"Who was Johnny?" I asked, picking absently at a crack in the wooden porch step.

"My baby!" Her voice held pride and love and something else. Sorrow?

"I didn't know you and Frank had a child."

She blinked, turning to me in surprise. "Oh . . . oh, yes. We had our Johnny in 1955. June 8, 1955." She recited the date with a bob of her head. "It was such a warm day. Or at least it seemed warm to me," she said with a chuckle. "I was already way past thirty, you know, and the doctor had always told me I'd never have a child. We . . . we were so happy when he was wrong."

"I can imagine," I said, warmed by the joy in Janet's expression.

"It wasn't easy, though," she went on, shaking her head at the memory. "The trip to the mainland never took so long, and it was still hours later before Johnny was born. Even then they had to take him."

"Cesarean?"

"No, no." She made a pinching motion with her right hand. "Forceps. Still, it was worth it. He was a charming boy."

In all innocence I asked, "Where is he now? Does he live nearby?"

Janet's lips compressed, and the corners of her mouth turned down. Without looking at me, she said flatly, as if she'd said it time and time again, "My boy is dead. Johnny is dead."

I went cold all over and cursed my own curiosity. Laying my hand on her arm, I whispered, "I'm so sorry, Janet. I had no idea."

She patted my hand, a weak smile on her lips. "I know, dear. It's not your fault. It all happened a very long time ago."

I wasn't sure what to say, and for a few moments we sat silently. Janet was lost in her memories, and I was imagining the tragic loss of a child. Was that what made Frank Peabody so bitter and reticent? Maybe he had never fully recovered.

"Would you like to see his picture?" Janet

asked suddenly in a bright tone. A mother's pride.

I hastened to accept. "I'd love to!"

She led the way back into the house and their suite of rooms off the kitchen. We walked into the tiny sitting room, plainly decorated with few homey touches. The sofa and two chairs had obviously begun their stay on the island in the other part of the house, eventually being demoted to their current location.

Janet motioned me to a seat on the worn floral sofa and went over to a battered but still lovely wooden chest. The ornate gold handles were tarnished with age, but the drawer slid open smoothly. Carefully she withdrew an old leather-bound photo album nearly a foot wide.

She heaved a heavy sigh and settled beside me, running her hands lovingly over the gold embossing on the cover. "I haven't looked at these in years," she stated in happy anticipation, opening the album.

First we looked at pictures of the much younger Peabodys on their wedding day. Janet wore a simple long gown and a broad smile. Frank, barely recognizable, looked severe in his suit. His dark hair gleamed smooth and slick, and his eyes were alight with happiness. They stood side by side in front of a big black car. Janet clutched a small bouquet.

"We had a lovely wedding. Wasn't Frank handsome?" She leaned closer to the photo, squinting at the faces.

"Oh, yes," I said honestly, wondering where that man had gone.

She turned several more pages, narrating each snapshot. The colors were faded now, the faces standing out in stark white. Then came the baby pictures. First a shot of little John Peabody in the hospital. A tiny, knitted cap covered his head, riding just above his eyebrows. Beneath it, his huge eyes looked into the camera serenely. He had sweet chubby cheeks, and his lips were pursed in a kiss.

"He's adorable," I cooed and Janet did, too, beaming at her little boy.

More pictures followed. Father and son, mother and child. In the pram, in the garden, under the Christmas tree. Then, abruptly, the images ran out. The empty pages began just after the Christmas shots, and I knew the baby's death must have occurred at that time. After looking at all the old pictures and hearing the stories, I felt as if I'd known Johnny. Hesitantly I asked, "What happened?"

Janet closed the album before answering.

"It was about six months after Andrew had come to live here. He and Johnny were nearly the same age when it happened. Just eighteen months old. It was winter, and we were all out on the ice. Mr. Roland and Frank were skating. I had the boys bundled up on the sled Frank had made special. It was a lovely day. Warm for January." Her face creased quickly into a grimace. "Maybe that should have warned us. We'd had several nice days in a row. But the sun was shining, and the ice was smooth in the cove. . . ." Her voice trailed off. She was seeing the past again, I knew.

Shaking her head, she went on in a rush. "It all happened so fast. They were skating, and we were on the ice nearby, watching. Then there was a creak and a groan from all around us. It was as if the ice were alive! It just broke! Everywhere, it was cracking. We panicked, of course, trying to get to shore. I ran so fast, pulling the sled, but my feet! They slipped. One minute the boys were behind me. The next, the rope was just snatched from my hands, and the sled was gone. Gone!" The last words were no more than a whisper.

"When I turned around, the blades of the sled were showing through the churning water. So dark! So cold! And my babies

158

were down there! I jumped right in. Mr. Roland and Frank came over, shouting. Frank stayed on the ice, but Mr. Roland dived in. I'm afraid I wasn't much help. I'd managed to grab the hood on one of the boys' snowsuits, and I just held on and screamed. Mr. Roland went down several times. The cord on the sled had gotten tangled around the boys, trapping them down there. Eventually — it seemed like ages — he surfaced with Andrew, all limp and blue. Frank grabbed him and raced for shore. Mr. Roland was exhausted by then, and I just couldn't hold on any longer either. We tried! Oh, we tried!"

Her voice broke with a sob, and I hurried to put my arms around her. She buried her face in her hands, her fragile shoulders shaking. When she looked up at me, tears sparkled in her eyes. I blinked back my own. There was no need for her to finish the story.

"We never even found him," Janet cried in distress. "Not even in the spring. It was awful enough losing him, but to never see him —" Taking a deep, ragged breath, she squared her shoulders, patted my hand. "I'm all right, dear. It's just hard to think about."

Impulsively I gave her a big hug and said,

"I can't even imagine how bad it must have been. You were very brave."

"No, no. I wasn't quite brave enough."

I knew Janet was thinking of the son she couldn't save. She must have blamed herself for the tragedy, even though it wasn't her fault; must have carried that guilt with her every day for all these years. I gave a shudder as the vision of the cove appeared: not as I'd seen it on a calm summer day, but in winter, the water black beneath the ice, the sky low and threatening. Haunting.

"It took a long time to get over, if you ever get over something so awful," Janet said. "Every winter I look at that ice and remember it all."

"Frank too?"

She gave a quick nod. "Yes. But he'd never admit it. He gets angry if I even bring it up." Her eyes darted around the room. "That's why there are no pictures of Johnny here. Frank won't allow it."

"You don't mind that?" I asked, thinking it cruel of Frank to take away all that remained of Johnny Peabody.

She shrugged. Placing her hands near her heart, she smiled. "I have my memories."

"Janet!" A voice bellowed from the kitchen, startling me by its volume. Frank didn't seem the kind to raise his voice. I would have pegged him the silent, sulky type.

Janet scrambled to her feet, clutching her photo album protectively. She didn't answer, but scurried over to replace the album in its drawer. As she was turning away, the sitting-room door opened.

Frank stood framed in the doorway, his hand still on the knob. Janet looked like a child with her hand in the cookie jar, caught in the act. Her voice quavered as she said, "Hello, dear. We were just having some girl talk." She tipped her head in my direction, and I wanted to crawl behind the sofa to escape Frank's baleful glare. Up until she pointed me out, he hadn't seen me.

"Hmph! You!" he muttered angrily.

The thin courtesy smile I'd been attempting slipped from my face. Looking hot and angry in his scuffed overalls, Frank turned his attention to Janet. Perhaps it was her proximity to the drawer of photo albums or my presence or the frightened look on his wife's face, but he rapidly realized what we'd been up to. His scowl darkened.

"You been talking about the boy!" he accused.

Janet paled. "We . . . we were just visiting," she said. "That's all."

Frank's big, callused hand came out, one

long finger wagging at Janet. "I don't want talk of the boy. It's past! It's done! Leave it be!"

"But, Frank —"

"No!" He wheeled around, pausing just long enough to send a hateful glance in my direction. The door slammed shut behind him. A picture on one wall tipped to one side from the force.

My eyes went to Janet, but she wouldn't look at me. Hurrying over to set the picture right, she said faintly, "I'm sorry about that. Frank can be excitable."

I knew she was embarrassed, so I tried to make it easy for her. "And men say women are the emotional ones." I tried for a lighthearted tone, but it didn't quite ring true.

Janet turned from the picture and smiled. "Thanks for the visit, Sarah. It was lovely. I'm glad I got to talk about Johnny. When you just carry a thing around inside you, it hurts too much."

She opened her arms and I stepped right in, stooping down to return her hug.

"I'd better get back to work," I said, genuinely reluctant to leave.

"Yes," she agreed. "We don't want you to be in trouble too."

She followed me back into the kitchen, and we parted at the door.

Chapter Twelve

There followed several days of gloomy weather. Cloudy skies and thunderstorms moved in, breaking up the sunny streak we'd been having. The television said farmers were dancing in their fields, welcoming the rain. In a way I welcomed it too. It meant little distraction from my work. The end was in sight now, and that quickened my pace.

On the third rainy morning, I walked along the darkened hall to the library, carrying my after-breakfast coffee and yawning. It would have been easy to just go back to bed, in all truth. It was nearly as dark as night outside.

I unlocked the library doors and pushed them open, reaching for the light switch at the same time. When I turned to face the room, I gave a gasp.

Books were scattered everywhere. Torn from the newly ordered shelves and hurled onto the floor, they were strewn drunkenly around the ransacked room. All the papers from my desk were confetti on the floor. The desk lamp lay on its side, shade askew.

Heart pounding, I hurried over to my desk, setting down my coffee cup and wrenching open the desk drawer. Nestled inside, untouched, were the catalog cards I'd spent the last few weeks drawing up. I let out a tense breath. At least that portion of my work had been spared. Whoever had done this either hadn't known about the cards or didn't care.

As I moved slowly around the room, picking up the books and examining them for damage, I realized the perpetrator of this job must not have wanted to destroy the library. Otherwise, the books would have been slashed, the cards destroyed. The windows could have been left open to the storm.

No, bad as it was, it seemed as if this were just surface damage. I'd have to spend the whole day setting the place to rights again, but the setback would end there.

Was this a warning to me? The thought chilled me and I shivered, glancing nervously around as the rain increased its tempo against the window.

There was only one person I knew of on the island who made no attempt to hide his animosity. One man who, just a few days earlier, had looked at me with anger blazing in his eyes. One man. Frank Peabody.

A flash of lightning lit the sky, sending

the garden into stark relief. In that instant I saw him. Head down against the rain, his slicker glistening wet, Frank limped along in the direction of the woods. He didn't glance up, and, as fast as it had come, the light was gone. The garden lay in darkness as thunder drummed overhead.

I bit my lip hard as nervous tension took hold, making me want to scream at the top of my lungs or burst into tears. Or both. Unsteadily I reached for my coffee cup, drinking down the lukewarm stuff without tasting it. What should I do next? I wondered, pressing my hands around the cup. Tell someone or tell no one? Run to Richard? Call the cops? Wait for Andrew to surface? One alternative careened after the next through my buzzing mind.

Righting the desk chair, I sank onto its smooth surface, pulling one sneakered foot up underneath me. Then I decided. As soon as Andrew returned, I would tell him about this incident. In the meantime I'd clean up the mess and keep my mouth shut. If I told Richard and confided my suspicions as to the culprit, he might just try to confront Frank. After seeing Frank's anger with Janet, the last thing I wanted was to provoke a confrontation. Yes, the path of least resistance looked pretty appealing at the moment. I'd tell the boss and no one else.

I sighed and set down my cup with a thump. There was no time to waste now if I wanted the place back in order before anyone happened along the hallway. As a precaution against interruptions, I locked the library doors — this time from the inside. Pushing up the sleeves on my sweatshirt, I marched back into the room, wondering how someone could do so much damage without waking up the entire household. Another unwelcome mystery.

I paused at lunchtime just long enough to grab an apple from the fruit bowl in the dining room and a soda from the kitchen fridge. Passing Richard in the hall, I waved my apple but didn't stop to chat. Instead, he came after me.

"No lunch today?" he asked.

I smiled weakly, tossing my apple from one hand to the other and avoiding his gaze. "Nope. I'm on a roll."

Tipping his head to one side, he said, "You must be. There's dirt on your cheek."

I rubbed at the spot he indicated and shrugged. "Tote that barge, lift that bale!" I teased. "That's me!" While he stood staring, I turned and fled, calling over one shoulder, "See you!"

My sneakers slapped on the shiny tiles of the hallway as I ran along. I didn't feel like making conversation. I couldn't talk to anyone just now. Least of all to Richard. Not now. Maybe not ever. Tears caught at my throat and burned my eyes at the thought. But the facts couldn't be avoided.

While I was putting the library back together again, the reason for the attack had become obvious. At least a dozen more books were now missing.

Closing the library doors behind me and locking them tight, I leaned up against the cool glass for an instant. It was impossible to collect my thoughts when my emotions were all caught up in the fray. I tried to be logical. Reasonable. But that didn't waylay my fears. It increased them.

Over the weeks I'd spent on the island, I'd gotten very familiar with the library collection. After all, I'd sorted them, cataloged them, cleaned them, and checked them against the old inventory. By now I knew what books were there — especially the very special ones. I could tick off on my fingers those rare first editions I'd handled so carefully.

And now, just as certainly, I could name the ones missing. This random violence was engineered to confuse me, to prevent me from seeing the crime. At least for a little while.

The suspects were few. After all, Andrew was still away, and he'd have no reason to ransack his own belongings. Richard had pointed a finger at Frank in regard to the missing paintings, but I couldn't accept the doddering old man as art thief and rare-book fiend.

Of course, I also couldn't accept the only other alternative.

But who else besides Richard had a working knowledge of the book market? Had connections with book dealers? Had the opportunity to commit the crime?

The answer to my questions drummed over and over in my brain like a dream sequence in an old B movie.

Richard. Richard. Richard.

Rather than stand motionless and think, I decided action might help distract me and set to work on the books again. I worked feverishly, checking for damage and reshelving them without even being aware of the process.

As I did, the images of our times together passed before me like a slide show. Our lazy evening strolls, cuddling together on the sofa, the trip to Rifkin, kissing in the darkened warehouse. And all the while he'd been a thief! My face flushed with embarrassment and anger. I felt like a fool, being used so cruelly. It was a horrible thing to do, entangling my heart without meaning a word of that sweet wooing. Blinding my eyes by kissing them shut!

He was beyond contempt, I thought, angrily shoving a book back on its shelf. He didn't deserve my respect or my love.

As my fury built, so did the case against Richard. It was easy to see that the trip to Rifkin had been to set up the sale of more pilfered books. That story about the missing paintings could have been a lie! And if the paintings were gone, I was pretty sure Frank Peabody hadn't been the man to spirit them away. It was simple to cast suspicion on the old man. Simple and smart.

"How could you?" I muttered, amazed at Richard's audacity and my own gullible nature. But my self-esteem, in shreds by this time, put up one small protest I couldn't ignore.

What if it all hadn't been a lie? Could the part about us be true? Could he really care for me, even if he were a thief? My hand stopped on its way to another shelf. Right now I wasn't ready to question whether I wanted a thief to love me. Just whether Richard did. Remembering the feel of his lips on mine, of being held in his arms, I knew only one thing for certain. For good or bad I loved him.

Because of the rain, evening seemed to come much earlier that night. By dinnertime I had the library nearly back in order and felt ready for a long, well-deserved nap. Pressing the heels of my hands against my eyes, I debated going in to dinner. Having to be so close to Richard when I was full of doubts and questions wouldn't be conducive to easy digestion. At just the thought, my stomach gave a low warning rumble. Or maybe I was just hungry.

Taking a last look around the room and finding all signs of the morning catastrophe gone, I unlocked the doors and let myself out, then locked them once again.

There was a surprise waiting in the dining room.

I arrived a few moments late to find Andrew reigning at the head of the table. He looked tired and nervous. Those blue eyes were dimmed, with dark circles beneath them, making his face appear sunken and old. A five o'clock shadow was visible on his cheeks — unthinkable in the usually fastidious man.

He greeted me with a weary smile and

chattered on all through the meal. He and Richard talked about sports and the upcoming football season. I spent the time planning what I would say to Andrew after dinner. I would not come right out and accuse anyone. I'd simply report the situation and let him draw his own — the only — conclusion.

As we were finishing dessert, Richard reached for my hand beneath the table and gave it a squeeze. I felt that squeeze around my heart as well. I turned the tight line of my mouth into a brief smile.

"Could we go for a stroll, now that the rain has stopped?" he asked.

I glanced out the window and realized he was right. The storm had passed. I couldn't even say when. But it must have been over for some time, I reasoned, because Andrew had to come across the water. The idea of the *Molly Jane* on a choppy lake made me queasy.

"No." I shook my head and motioned in Andrew's direction. "I . . . I have to speak to Andrew about the library. I thought I'd catch him after dinner." I looked away from Richard, down at my hands, tightly clasped in my lap. "It's kind of important."

"Oh, okay. Well, maybe later." He turned back to the strawberry cheesecake, sounding puzzled and hurt. His tone tore at my heart.

I didn't want to hurt him. I wanted to be wrong. I wanted Frank Peabody to be the guilty man. But Richard was the logical choice. He had the knowledge and the opportunity. Nothing would make me happier than to have Andrew explain my worries away, providing me with an answer to the puzzle without breaking my heart.

When Andrew got up to leave the table, I followed him out of the room, catching up to him in the hall.

"May I see you for a moment?" I asked, my hand clutching his arm, my voice betraying my nerves by shaking.

Andrew frowned, his eyes lost in shadows.

"It's something you need to know," I added, hoping he wouldn't be angry at my interruption. "About the library."

"Of course, Sarah. Of course." He looked up and down the hall, as if deciding where we could go. "The conservatory?" he suggested and I nodded, following silently as he led the way.

I hadn't been in this room before and gave it only a cursory glance now, unable to see clearly with only weak moonlight for illumination. It smelled of the rich, dark soil, moist and heady. The fragrance of the flowers was gentle, subtle, very much like the garden out back. The plants grew in wonderful abundance, reflecting in the glass as dark shadows.

Andrew pressed a button, and dim lights appeared, hidden among the foliage, enabling us to see each other without destroying the natural atmosphere. Suddenly I wished I were anywhere else.

"Well? What is it?" His words were sharp, but his tone was merely impatient. He must be tired after his business trip, and nearly the minute he'd gotten home, I was making him address problems. Perhaps this had been a poor bit of timing.

"You said this had to do with the library?" Now he was leading me into the topic. It was too late to turn back.

I reached out to touch a glossy, smooth leaf on one of the plants, feeling its surface beneath my trembling fingers. Taking a deep breath, I began. Ten minutes later he'd heard the facts. The missing books, the ransacked library, Emil Fincher's shop.

When I mentioned Emil and finding one of Roland's books in his shop, Andrew's eyebrows shot up and, even in the dim light, I could see his discomfiture. After I'd said my piece, confided my suspicions that someone on the island — I didn't speculate as to who — was stealing Andrew blind, there was a long silence.

With a sigh, Andrew turned away from me and walked across the room, bending down to sniff a blossom here and there in an absentminded way. Finally he said, "I don't know what to tell you, Sarah. This is pretty startling news. Do you have any idea who the criminal is?"

I was glad he wasn't looking at me then. It was easier to lie to his back. "No," I said, my voice low and soft. "I have no idea."

Clouds passed over the moon outside, and the room dimmed accordingly. Andrew was just a black silhouette now, motionless in the night. The only sound was a faint trickling of water from somewhere. The sprinklers? The rooftop? Sounds seemed amplified in the conservatory, making it difficult to tell where they came from.

"The police should be contacted, I suppose," Andrew said, his voice dull and resigned. His hands were fists resting on his hips in that King of Siam pose I'd seen before.

"And the insurance company," I added. "I realize money won't bring the books back, but it's all you'd have now."

"Hmm." He nodded slowly, thoughtfully, and turned to face me. The clouds passed and the moon spread its glow once again.

Coming from behind him, it lit up Andrew's hair, while his face remained concealed by shadow. "Yes, well, today money is everything, you know." The words were cold, and I realized that's all the books were to him — money on a shelf. He didn't seem to care about their history, their rarity, their reflection of the world. He only cared about their monetary value.

"I'll have to give this some thought, Sarah, but if what you say is true, it's definitely a case for the authorities." His hands clenched at his sides. "I will not be deprived of what's mine! I am Roland's heir. The books are mine! The house is mine! Everything in it is mine!" His voice had risen with each sentence, like a snowball rolling downhill out of control, or a two-year-old throwing a tantrum.

He stepped nearer to me, close enough so he could look into my eyes. I swallowed nervously over the lump in my throat and crossed my arms in front of me to keep him from coming even closer.

"I'm nobody's fool, Sarah," he hissed in a whisper. "Whoever is responsible for this will be dealt with. Harshly." His breath was warm on my face, he was so close now. His eyes blazed with fury, and I pitied Richard when he was found out. The man before me had no mercy.

Abruptly the fire of rage vanished from Andrew's eyes, replaced by another kind of fire I liked even less. His hands reached out to touch my arms, gently, but without hesitation. "Thank you for telling me, Sarah," he said in honeyed tones. "I'm grateful for your trust and your honesty. You're a special person." He ran his hands up my arms to my shoulders, pulled me nearer. "And a beautiful one."

Before I could break this embrace, his lips were on mine, harsh and demanding. The sharp whiskers on his cheeks scratched my face. The suddenness of his approach dazed me and caught me off guard. I remained rigid in his arms, refusing to be drawn in by his kiss, fighting the wave of fear that threatened to engulf me.

When had this happened? What made him think I wanted his kisses and attention?

Unbidden, the feel of Richard's kisses overwhelmed me. The warmth and tenderness we shared was utterly absent here. Andrew was the boss, domineering and in control. No give-and-take. No consideration for anyone but himself. No!

Pushing against his chest with both hands, I turned away. "Please!" I whispered. "Don't."

Andrew's grasp tightened on my shoulders. He held me firm when I would have bolted from the room. "Don't?" he echoed. He gave me a shake, forcing me to look at him, and repeated, "Don't?"

Scarcely breathing, I nodded, squaring my shoulders in false bravado. "You heard me."

Releasing me so quickly I rocked backward, he held up both hands in surrender. A mocking smile, insincere and patronizing, played over his lips. "Can't blame me for trying, Sarah. And I'll try again," he warned.

I backed slowly in the direction of the door, putting space between us before turning to run from the room. The echo of his laughter followed me, but I gave it no thought. All I wanted was to get away. The sanctuary of my room beckoned, and I hurried down the hallway and ran blindly up the staircase, tears of frustration and anger blurring my sight. I turned the corner at the top of the stairs into the wing I shared with Richard, sobbing outright.

This was all Richard's fault. The thieving, the confrontation with Andrew, the deepening crack that was slowly breaking my heart. I gave his door a malevolent look as I passed, fumbling in my pocket for the key to my room. It took me a few moments to find it. I inserted the tiny key in the lock

177

with shaky hands, groaning aloud as I heard the door down the hall open.

"Sarah?" Richard stepped into the passageway, and I looked up, giving the key a violent turn.

"Go away!" I hissed between my teeth as tears ran unchecked down my cheeks. I registered his stunned look in the instant before I entered my room, slamming the door behind me.

Collapsing onto the bed, I let go, indulging the sobs I could no longer hold back. But my privacy didn't last long. In my haste I hadn't locked the bedroom door, and now it opened. Without looking up, I knew it was Richard and buried my face deeper into the pillows. I heard the door click shut again and knew we were alone in the room. What would he do when he knew I'd told Andrew about the crimes?

His hand on my shoulder was gentle, but I stiffened beneath his touch. "Sarah, what's wrong?"

I looked up, pulling away from his hands and scrambling rapidly to my feet. My stomach was tied in a heavy knot, and my heart burned with the pain of betrayal. "I know, Richard. I know about the books!" I spoke slowly, struggling to regain my composure, sniffing back my tears.

Reaching into his pocket, Richard withdrew a handkerchief and held it out to me, waving it at me when I didn't instantly accept it. He waited silently while I blew my nose. Across the room the mirror caught our reflections. My eyes were red and swollen, my cheeks blotchy from my tears. Richard stood near the dresser, looking ill at ease. He shifted from one foot to the other and said in a petulant tone, "What are you talking about?"

I whirled around to face him. "It's bad enough as it is, Richard. Don't even try to deny it."

"Would you mind explaining what crime I'm guilty of, Sarah? If you're going to condemn me, I'd like to know what for." He was angry; his very posture made that clear, even if his tone had not.

I gave a great sigh, my eyes sweeping around the room, taking in its details, flitting from the pictures on the walls to the porcelain doll that had been Richard's gift, sitting on the dresser top. Seeing the doll's charming expression, that hint of a smile curving her lips, I remembered the kiss that had followed that day in the warehouse and closed my eyes to block out the memory.

Nervously pleating the edge of Richard's hanky, I steeled myself for the confrontation ahead and spoke quickly, before I could lose my nerve. "Ransacking the library to cover up the theft was clever, Richard, but it didn't hide the crime for long. The most valuable books have vanished overnight." Discovering that the man I'd fallen in love with was a thief was bad enough. To have him insult my intelligence by denying the obvious was worse. I took a breath and went on, deliberately speaking slowly in poor imitation of patience. "It doesn't take a mental giant to figure out who knows all about rare books. Who knows book dealers. Who would know which books were worth the most money and where they could be easily sold off!"

Richard crossed his arms, leaning on one hip against the dresser, a smart-aleck look on his face. "You," he said.

I shook my head to clear out cobwebs, certain I hadn't heard correctly. "What?"

He mocked my tone in reply. "You know about rare books. You'd know which ones were worth the most. You know book dealers from all over the state. You must be the thief. If books are even missing."

"That's absurd!" I exploded, taking a step closer to him, the heat of anger rising in my face.

Richard's eyes caught mine, and I stopped

dead. For a moment we battled it out; then he said, "No more absurd than your accusation, Sarah."

I had to admit, he had a point. The arguments that had convinced me of his guilt could also be applied to me. But I knew I wasn't the thief, and if Richard wasn't, who was?

"I didn't do it!" I said in exasperation.

"Well, neither did I."

"Prove it!" I challenged.

Richard sighed. "What would you consider proof, Sarah? How can I convince you?" He stepped closer and held out his hand imploringly. "It's important that you believe me."

Without even realizing it, I curled my fingers around his. "And I want to believe you. But how did the *Historian's History* end up with Emil?" I jerked my head at the book, which lay faceup on the nightstand.

"A legitimate question." He dropped my hand and reached into his shirt pocket. "This should help. It was in the mail sack Andrew brought home with him tonight. The letter was addressed to me — I was expecting news of the paintings, you know. There's a P.S. for you." He held out an envelope with a Rifkin postmark. "It's from Emil," he added unnecessarily.

I removed the letter from the envelope and flipped it rapidly over to where Emil's signature was scrawled in spidery letters. Beneath it I read:

P.S. Please tell the charming Sarah her book has made an interesting journey. I received it with a lot from Jack Westerley, Inc., my dealer in South Clifton. He informed me his records claim the book was purchased six months ago from a man who called himself Pete Johnson. He asked to be paid in cash. Listed his residence as a rooming house in South Clifton. I asked Jack to check further and, according to him, this Johnson has been a regular customer since last fall. He's an older man who "looks like a farmer," in Jack's words. Walks with a limp, doesn't say much. Always wants cash and brings in less than a dozen volumes each time. Is this stolen merchandise, Richard? Certainly appears that way. Be careful and KEEP ME INFORMED.

I read it all over again and then a third time. A wave of something like relief went through me, and my heart seemed to start beating again.

When I looked up, Richard was watching me, and he didn't say, "I told you so." I said the first thing that came to mind.

"Frank Peabody."

Richard nodded. "That's what I thought. It seems pretty obvious, just from the description. When you add in the fact that he had plenty of opportunity, it looks like the only conclusion."

I crossed the room and sank down onto the chair near the window. "But why would he do it?" The letter hung limp between my fingers, and I fluttered it hopelessly. "I don't understand any of this. I don't know what to think or who to believe. I want to go home!" I whined, rubbing my forehead as if that would help my massive headache.

Richard took the letter from my hand and tucked it back into his pocket. "I never thought you were a quitter, Sarah."

I flipped my hair back behind my ear and shifted on the chair. "I'm not. You know that. I'm just so frustrated and angry and" — I hated to admit it — "a little bit frightened."

Richard clasped the back of the chair, sliding his hands back and forth across its satiny surface. "I don't blame you for being frightened. I don't know much about crimi-

183

nals, but the phrase 'armed and dangerous' comes to mind."

"Frank?" The word burst from me in astonishment.

Richard just nodded. "Go figure. If he's stealing things from his loyal employer, obviously he's gone over some edge. That isn't normal behavior. Once normal behavior stops, it seems to reason that anything could follow." He shook his head slowly from side to side. "Don't cross him, Sarah. Stay out of his way. We'll have to let the police take care of this situation."

"I've told Andrew. He said he'd contact the authorities tomorrow." I was ready to put this problem into the hands of anyone else. The police seemed the obvious choice. Still, something bothered me. I tapped my fingers against my jaw and thought.

Richard watched me patiently. "Well?" he prodded at last.

I shrugged. "It's gone. There was something bugging me. Something that just doesn't make any sense. I mean, makes even less sense than before," I added. "Do you think Janet knows about this?" The idea brought a pang to my heart. Dear little Janet. So trusting, so sincere. She'd had plenty of heartbreak in her life, and now it looked as though there were more to come.

"I don't think so. She would never condone such behavior. You know the way she dotes on Andrew. She'd never let anyone hurt him. Not even her own husband."

"Yes, yes. You're right, of course. She mustn't know." The need for a direct answer overwhelmed me. "Let's ask her!" I jumped to my feet, ready to head for the door.

Richard grabbed my arm as I went by. "Are you crazy? If she does know, it could be dangerous to tip your mitt. If she doesn't know, do you want to be the one to break her heart?"

We exchanged a look of deep understanding. "I don't want any broken hearts," I said softly.

Richard's eyes grew warm and inviting, lit by an inner glow that filled me with a fierce longing for the security of his arms. Reading my mind, he slipped them around me, and I made no protest.

"Are you convinced of my innocence, Sherlock?"

I let my head answer instead of my heart, although the response from both was the same. "Yes, Richard. I do believe you. Please forgive my doubting mind."

"In your place, I might have thought the same," he admitted. "But according to

Emil, the pilfering began months ago. Before I'd ever heard of Echo Moon Island. I'm exonerated."

"I know that now. And it's quite a relief."

"Wouldn't want to be my moll, hmm?" he teased, and I laughed for what felt like the first time in days. "Get some rest," he went on, kissing me tenderly on the forehead. "If anyone is going to ask Janet anything, it will be the authorities tomorrow."

I nodded. "All right. But you can't honestly expect me to sleep! I'll spend the whole night lying awake, listening for Frank, imagining him sneaking around in the dark." I shuddered. This was worse than reading ghost stories. This was real.

"Lock the door behind me," Richard ordered as he crossed the room.

"Don't worry. I'll put the chair under the doorknob too." I let him out into the shadowed hallway.

"Try to have sweet dreams, Sarah. Tomorrow could see this mystery solved."

I returned his kiss. "Let's hope so."

Richard waited in the hall until I had secured the lock and tilted the heavy chair beneath the knob. In no time I was under the covers, my knees pulled up to my chest as if to ward off the chill of anxiety. It must have been exhaustion that led me to sleep. My dreams were deep and elusive.

Chapter Thirteen

The next morning at breakfast, Andrew didn't appear. It was impossible to tell if he'd already left on the important errand of bringing in the police or if he'd just overslept.

Richard and I shared a companionable breakfast with Chuck and Joe. Their work, like mine, was drawing to a close, and it was obvious they'd be glad to leave Echo Moon Island behind. I couldn't join wholeheartedly in this unusually chatty meal, naturally. My eyes kept darting to the doorway, expecting — and fearing — the sight of Frank Peabody. Richard sensed my apprehension and, several times, gave my hand a reassuring squeeze.

"We've got to go down to the dock now," he told me, glancing at his watch. "The *Molly Jane* is due in with supplies, and we've got to go back for some things in the storehouse on the mainland besides." He gave a sigh. "This could take all day."

Across the table, Chuck and Joe rose slowly to their feet, draining their coffee cups in tandem and reflecting Richard's enthusiasm with grunts and groans. "I'll be along in a minute," Richard told them as they left the room.

Turning to me, he said, "Hang in there, Sarah. I know you've still got a burning desire to run to Janet and pump her for information."

I opened my mouth to protest. Oh, he was right. I was still eager to ferret out the truth, but the fact that he could read my mind made me eager to make him think he couldn't. "I know your approach is the safe one, Richard. I swear I won't ask any questions." My right hand shot up to make the promise even more sincere.

He smiled, the corners of his eyes creasing into fine lines. "I'm glad. The last thing I'd want would be to have you in jeopardy."

I laughed. "That's not something I'm eager to bring about, either, you know."

We went off in separate directions, although I'm sure our minds were on the same thing. It was hard to concentrate on my work when I kept one ear cocked for sounds from the hall, waiting for the arrival of Andrew and the police. After a few hours, with no sign of either, I shrugged and wondered aloud what was happening.

Having no one to talk to didn't stop me

from muttering my rambling thoughts as I cleaned and reshelved books. The task was purely mechanical, which was just what I needed. My brain refused to budge from the topic of the mystery, and I went over the things I knew for certain.

Frank had been selling off books from Roland Clayton's library for a period of over six months. He'd traveled all the way to South Clifton to do it, so obviously he feared discovery. Upon hearing of the thefts, Andrew had looked angry and concerned, but not surprised.

My rag stopped its motion across the cover of the book I held as I realized that truth. Andrew had not been surprised to learn his books were disappearing. I had suspected Richard of the crime, and perhaps Andrew did too. But it seemed more likely that, after knowing and living with the Peabodys for so long, he might immediately connect Frank's behavior with the trouble. Recalling the look I'd seen on Andrew's face as his anger had surfaced, I remembered the other times I'd seen traces of that look. Each time it had been when Andrew was discussing Frank. The tension between the two of them was palpable. I caught my lower lip between my teeth.

Could it be that Andrew did know of

the thefts and already knew Frank was responsible? If he did, though, why had he allowed it to go on? To protect Janet from the truth?

I resumed working, my thoughts moving in what appeared to be logical steps. My very first day on the island, Andrew had said he endured Frank's presence because of Janet and his affection for her. How much was he willing to overlook for her sake? Laziness, perhaps. Theft? I doubted it.

Rising from my chair, I carried the stack of newly cleaned books back to the shelf and aligned them carefully. I reached for the next batch on the shelf below, loading them into my arms and holding the top one in place with my chin. As I crossed the room, the precarious pile shifted, sliding out of my grasp. Instinctively I lurched toward the desktop, my hands moving in three directions at once, trying to clasp the books against my chest. My foot smashed into the leg of the desk as the books slipped away, careening noisily onto the desk, the chair, and the floor.

"Drat!" I exclaimed, hands on my hips in disgust. With a sigh I squatted down to retrieve the volumes that were strewn around me like petals blown off a bloom by the wind. My clumsy action had knocked the heavy old desk off the book Richard had placed beneath the leg weeks earlier. I reached for that thin red volume now, a sentimental smile on my lips as I remembered the incident. It was the first time we met, I thought, running my hand gently over the faded fabric cover of the book. I sat back on my heels and opened it more by rote than by design.

At first it appeared to be another accounts book. The yellowing pages were covered with tightly spaced writing. My eyes darted briefly over the words without taking them in. I wasn't really interested in the contents, after all. Then, as I turned another page, I noticed a brittle bit of newsprint lying loosely inside. One look at the headline made my feet go out from under me, leaving me sitting on the floor, agog with curiosity.

WINTER TRAGEDY AT ECHO MOON, it said. The date in the corner was January 29, 1957, and I knew in a flash it must be an account of the drowning that claimed the life of little Johnny Peabody.

Eighteen-month-old John Peabody drowned yesterday off the shore of Echo Moon Island. The tragedy occurred about 2 P.M. when the Peabody family was out on the ice with Roland Clayton, owner of the island, and his ward, two-year-old Andrew Clayton.

The article continued, but my eyes refused to move over the text. Even a dispassionate description of the accident couldn't lessen the horror of it, and I felt a wave of sympathy for Janet — and for Frank. Maybe the loss of his son had left him permanently unbalanced, leading to these more recent events.

I turned the scrap of newspaper over. There was nothing on the back but advertisements. Flipping to the beginning of the little red book, I scanned the writing, recognizing it now as the same writing in the inventory. Methodical, precise, and quite legible.

With a gasp, I realized I held Roland Clayton's diary in my hands. I glanced rapidly over my shoulder at the doors to the library, as if expecting someone to burst in and snatch the book away. It didn't belong here with his other books. It should be in with the family papers, wherever those were. For a moment I wondered if Roland had placed it here deliberately, knowing almost anyone could find it and read it. Wanting them to?

This theory certainly justified my burning itch to sit down with the book and read it beginning to end. *After all,* I reasoned, *perhaps it will give me some insight about Frank. Make sense of this confusion.* Part of my conscience kept up a squawk as I walked to the window seat and crawled in. The intermittent sunshine of early morning had evaporated, and a distinct gloom had settled outside. The garden was shadowed by clouds overhead, and it looked as if more rain were on the way.

The diary began just about the time Andrew Clayton's parents were killed. Roland described the boy's arrival in great detail, and beneath his words the pain he felt at the loss of his brother was clear. Since this was a diary, originally intended for the eyes of only the author, it was honest and straightforward. Roland seemed a man of great emotion, with a strong sense of family. He viewed his responsibility to the child Andrew as: *the very least I can do for my dear little brother. His child shall be my child, with all the love and happiness I can give him. My immeasurable sorrow may be salved just a fraction by the presence of this charming lad. He is so like his father.*

Tears pricked at my eyes as I read these words. The next pages continued the story.

Roland mentioned Johnny Peabody often, since both boys were in Janet's care and they were constant playmates. In no time I'd reached the month of the accident. There was no entry for that time, just a blank page with yellowed spots where tape had once held the newspaper in place. The next entry was dated six months later, and I remembered Janet telling me how hard Roland had taken Johnny's death.

August 10 1957: That demanding woman from the historical society keeps hounding me about allowing Echo Moon to be included in their next pamphlet. Local land-mark, indeed! Can no one recognize my grief, my mourning over the loss of that dear child? I'll not permit my island to become a stop on a map for curiosity seekers, even if they veil their gawking by labeling it "history"!

The words were written with a heavy hand, scrawled quickly and in anger. The paper had bent under the pressure of the pen and was now ridged with each line. Entries that followed reaffirmed Roland's sorrow, and it became apparent he held himself responsible for the accident, much as Janet did. He wrote:

If only I'd not insisted on the outing! An-
drew would not be alone in the nursery.
Janet continues to dress him in Johnny's
clothing and insists on calling him Johnny
too. I've asked her — begged her — not
to continue this way, but she is adamant.
I still think it best that we accept the situ-
ation as it is, but she refuses. Stubborn
woman!

I took a deep breath, my hands shaking
as I turned the page, imagining the household in turmoil. How long had it been before Janet had been able to accept Johnny's
death? She had not mentioned this identity
problem when she told me of the accident.
Perhaps after all this time she had forgotten.

I flipped rather rapidly through several
years' worth of entries, until Frank's name
jumped out at me. My hand stilled on the
page, and I leaned forward.

June 16, 1959: A wonderful day. The first
we've seen of summer. Took the boy down
to the cove for a spot of fishing — much
to Frank's disapproval. I don't know what
is wrong with that man. His attitude this
afternoon was most disturbing. When he
heard of my plans, the look he gave me
was truly hateful. He is very possessive of

Andrew, of course. Ever since the accident I've noticed he's taken a greater interest in the child. Understandable, I suppose, and yet I find myself resenting it. We'll have to have a chat. He needs to remember who is in charge here and how quickly I could end his idyllic life on the island.

Chewing absently on my lower lip, I read the paragraph a second time. Frank was angry at Roland. Roland threatened Frank. An employer can always fire an employee, but somehow Roland's words did not seem so harmless. I turned the page and read further.

Maybe he has forgotten where my netsuke collection came from, but I have not. I could have turned him in that night at Hamilton's when he stole it. When I found him shot and bleeding in the back of my car.

The book dropped out of my hands as I jumped, not believing the words before me. I clapped it against my legs before it hit the floor and hurriedly scrambled to find my place. As I riffled through the pages, a tightly folded piece of paper fluttered out and drifted to my feet. Absently I retrieved

it, tucking it into a pocket before returning
to my reading.

*Yes, Frank was happy enough to do as I
said then. He dropped out of sight by coming here, safe from that long arm of the
law. And I got the netsuke, complete with
false ownership papers. But even that pales
in comparison to the real treasure Frank
brought me. Ah, Janet! What would my
life have been without you to care for me?
I shudder to think. . . .*

The entry ended, and I covered the page
with my hand as my thoughts raced. He
certainly was fond of Janet, but what was
all that about Frank? Apparently the thefts
here on Echo Moon were not his first venture into crime. I could picture the netsuke
collection glowing in its cabinet down the
hall. I had no idea who this man Hamilton
was, but his property was lovingly stored
here on Echo Moon. Stolen property.

"Curiouser and curiouser," I murmured,
wondering what other tales this diary would
tell.

Turning back to the book, I read on,
quickly skimming over the years that followed. Hard as I tried, I couldn't find any
further mention of Frank's past. There were

plenty of complimentary remarks about Janet, though, and I began to think Roland must have had a serious infatuation for her. Andrew's exploits and triumphs at home and at school were also diligently recorded. Roland Clayton had been a thorough chronicler, as well as a proud uncle. The book ended when Andrew was still a child, and I wondered if Roland had begun another volume. If it existed, it wasn't in this library. Of that I could be certain.

A rumble of thunder shook me from my ponderings, and I glanced swiftly out the window. Off in the distance, the sky was black and heavy with rain. Even now the first drops began to fall, pelting the window with a rhythmic thump, slow and steady. Another afternoon soaker, it seemed.

I closed the book and set it beside me, turning the events in Echo Moon's past over and over in my mind. For the first time I thought of the infant Andrew and his own close brush with death. How much of that could he possibly recall? Had that experience changed him in any permanent way? But, of course, my degree was in library science, not psychology, so my questions were doomed to remain unanswered.

Since my wristwatch showed noon, I decided to venture into the dining room —

not out of hunger, unless it was the hunger for information. Where was Andrew? Where were the police?

Neither were downstairs, I discovered soon enough. In fact, the only sounds throughout the house seemed to be made by my feet. I paused in the doorway of the dining room. The table was set, but there was no one else there to partake of the meal.

Richard and the workmen must still be away, I figured. They couldn't possibly be at the supply boat in this storm. Perhaps they had gotten stranded on the mainland. Lightning flashed, followed almost at once by an ear-shattering thunderclap.

With an attempt at nonchalance, I wandered into the kitchen. I had absolutely no intention of asking Janet any questions other than "Where is everybody?" My promise to Richard remained secure.

"Hello!" I called, pushing open the kitchen door. "Anybody home?"

Janet looked up from the cookbook she had spread across the table. Many more were opened and stacked on one another. "Oh, Sarah! You're looking for your lunch!" She pushed back her chair and rose swiftly. "I just lost all track of time. I'm trying to decide which dessert to try for dinner." She gestured at the glossy photos in the books and grinned. "They all look so good."

I tilted my head to view the key lime pie in the book nearest me. "Mmm. They certainly do!" I agreed, trying to keep my voice casual, although it was hard to look at her in the same way now.

Janet tied on an apron as she spoke. "What would you like for your lunch? Salad? Casserole? Soup?"

"Soup will be fine, if it's not too much trouble."

She scoffed at the thought. "No trouble at all."

I sawed thick slices of freshly baked bread from the still-warm loaf while Janet ladled soup, chock full of vegetables, into a heavy earthenware bowl. When she moved to carry the dish into the dining room, I intercepted her.

Taking the bowl from her hands, I set it on the kitchen table and said, "May I eat in here with you? It's kind of dreary and lonely in there today." I jerked my head in the direction of the other room. "I don't like to eat alone at the best of times. And this weather! It makes the very idea unbearable."

Cheeks dimpling, Janet waved me into one of the chairs. "Well, of course I can understand that, Sarah. It's a dreadful day." She settled back in across from me, pulling the cookbook a little bit closer. She studied recipes while I ate.

"What about this one?" she asked, spinning a book around to face me. She jabbed a gnarled old finger at a picture of something called peanut-butter fudge cake. My teeth hurt just looking at it.

"Maybe something a little lighter?" I suggested, my hand going to my stomach. "I've already put on enough weight since I came here," I teased.

Janet gave a laugh, shaking her head and turning another page.

Glancing over the array of titles scattered across the surface of the table, my eyes lit on a familiar sight. The *Happy Hubby* cookbook was half hidden beneath a newer, more colorful culinary encyclopedia. I reached for it hesitantly.

I finished my soup, pushing the bowl out of my way, and drew the book closer. Lifting the cover, I kept one eye on Janet, remembering how she had snatched this book away from me on that earlier occasion. Would she do the same now?

I skimmed past the chapters on appetizers and breads, riffling the dry, yellowed pages and hoping to see once more the photograph of the two little boys. As I expected, however, it was no longer there. I opened my mouth and shut it again. I would not ask any questions. I would not wonder aloud why the cookbook had been in the library. I would not —

"How do you suppose this book ended up in the library before?" I heard the words without realizing at first that I had spoken them. They hung in the air like the rain clouds, unwelcome and unexpected.

When I looked up, Janet was frowning, as if she were puzzled. Bravely, I showed her the cover illustration.

"Happy Hubby?" I prodded.

For an instant she caught my eye; then her gaze darted away. "Oh, yes," she said, her attempt at a casual tone offset by a slight tremor in her voice. "In the library? That was strange, hmm?"

In for a penny, I thought, and pushed what I hoped was my advantage. "You put it there, right? Hiding the picture from Frank. Did he see you with it? Or did he almost see you with it?"

Janet's head jerked up, her wide eyes looking at me in fear, and I knew I must be close to the truth. The scene developed in my mind. Janet, lost in memories of her boys, being startled by the arrival of Frank, as she'd been that day I had been with her.

"It was nothing, really," Janet said now,

attempting to dismiss the topic. Absently bending and unbending the corner of a page, she went on. "I'd been looking at that picture you saw. It was taken on the day of the accident, you know. Just before —" She stopped, pressing her eyes tightly shut and pausing before going on. "Anyway, I heard Frank coming and, well, you saw how he is about Johnny, so I hid the picture in that book. Frank . . . Frank thought that particular photo had been destroyed long ago. Couldn't bear the sight of it. I knew if he saw it again, he'd tear it up. My pictures are all I have. I couldn't let him take one away from me." She smoothed out the page she'd been mutilating before continuing. "The next time I had a chance to be in the library — taking tea to Mr. Roland — I took the book along. Slid it on a shelf when he wasn't looking. I thought it would be safe there. And it was."

"Until we spotted it," I put in and was rewarded with a faint, humorless smile.

"Yes. Until then."

"Where is the picture now? Hidden somewhere else?"

"Of course."

Our eyes met, mine curious, hers determined. I knew she'd never confide the secret, and, actually, there was no need for me to know. We were on the topic I wished to discuss, and that was sufficient.

Richard's words of warning came briefly to mind, but I stamped them down. We were just chatting. Nothing more. Honest.

"I've found something else," I told her. "Something pretty interesting."

She quirked an eyebrow, obviously anxious to hear what it was, and I went on matter-of-factly. "Roland's diary for the years around the accident."

Her eyes widened. For an instant it seemed her fair skin grew even paler. Then, abruptly, red spots bloomed in her cheeks. "Oh, dear," she said at last with a long, resigned sigh. "What does it say?"

I closed the *Happy Hubby* book and rested my elbows on its cover. It wasn't easy to answer. My last wish was to cause her pain, but I needed to know the truth. The circumstances of the past directly influenced the future. The situation on Echo Moon all those years ago could have a direct bearing on what was happening now. It could explain Frank's behavior. Before I spoke, I wondered fleetingly if Janet knew of her husband's criminal leanings. Richard had been right, I decided with a pang. I should have kept my mouth shut. These were dangerous waters.

"It's mostly about Andrew, of course," I said. "But there is plenty about Johnny, as well. Even after the tragedy."

Janet bobbed her head, one hand going back to pat gray hairs absently into place.

"I know you said Roland took Johnny's death especially hard. And that Frank was also deeply affected." I stretched my hand across the table to cover hers. "But you've never really told me how you felt." The words came out softly, inviting confidences. She offered none but sat silently, her hand motionless under mine. "I'm sure it was a horrible shock," I went on. "Enough to push even the strongest person off kilter. That's understandable."

"What are you saying, Sarah?" Janet's voice broke in on the end of my sentence. She looked up, working her hand out, away from my touch. "Are you implying I went off my rocker?" Her indignation was apparent in her tone. She sat bolt upright, facing me, something close to anger printed on her features.

"Of course not!"

"What then?"

"Roland's diary says. . . . Well, he says you called Andrew by Johnny's name. Dressed him in Johnny's clothes. Did you?"

Licking her lips nervously, Janet squirmed

in her chair. "What if I did?" she asked. "What's the harm in it?"

A good question.

"Curiosity killed the cat, Sarah," Janet warned.

I flinched under her scrutiny. "I know it seems as if I'm being nosy. But I have good reasons."

Janet's chair screeched backward, and she rose in one swift motion. "I don't want to hear your reasons, Sarah. Frank warned me to be quiet. 'Don't be so friendly,' he said. 'Don't trust any of them,' he said. Seems to me he was right this time. I'm disappointed." Her voice dropped off. There was an instant of silence before she added, "I did trust you."

"Then trust me now, when I tell you it's important for me to know." I stood up, too, looking across the wide wooden table at this tiny woman who had known such loss. Who might be in for more heartbreak, if my suspicions were correct.

"No, no, no!" she said, her voice high and thin. Her hands went to her ears, attempting to block out my words. "There is nothing you must know. Nothing! Go back to that library and leave me alone. Please!" She rested her hands on the table, letting them support her, looking old and frail.

I was taken with an inner battle, my own growing affection for Janet at war with all those questions I had. She might view my interest as mere curiosity, or worse. She could picture me as one of those people who linger at the scenes of accidents, filled with a morbid need to view the wreckage. The idea sent a chill of revulsion through me. I wanted to take her by the shoulders and look into her eyes, confessing my thoughts and my fears. Instead, I looked away, my fingers picking nervously at the cover of the book that began it all. At last, I said, "I'm sorry. It's thoughtless of me to be so insistent. You're right. It's none of my business what happened then. Or what happens now."

I turned to leave, not wishing to anger her further. She was facing away from me, rattling dishes around in the sink. I had my hand on the door when she said, "Whatever you're thinking, Sarah, you're wrong. I was upset by the baby's death, naturally. I cried for weeks. Even thought of jumping into that lake after him, as if I could exchange my life for his."

Stepping back into the room, I waited for her to go on. She wasn't looking at me. Wouldn't or couldn't, I didn't know.

At last she said, "But I always knew who

I was and where I was and what was true. If Mr. Roland's book says otherwise, well, I can't explain it." It seemed as if she put an extra emphasis on the pronoun. With a cup in one hand, she wheeled around, catching my eye and holding it with a fierce intensity. "Maybe you should trust me now."

The creak of the back door opening broke into our conversation. Janet shot a glance over her shoulder. The uneven thud of work boots in the hallway identified the intruder as Frank. She spared a second to look once more at me, poised on the doorjamb for flight. "Please," was all she said.

I bobbed my head in assent and slipped noiselessly from the room. As I walked slowly back toward the library, my mind worked feverishly.

Janet had said she'd dealt with her grief. Roland's diary said she had had trouble accepting things. Of course, I reasoned, either one of them could be wrong. Maybe Janet had actually reacted more strongly than she realized and Roland was correct. Perhaps Janet had been acting in a normal grieving pattern and Roland had simply misinterpreted. There seemed to be no way to know.

I returned to my desk in the library, shuffled some papers out of the way and cleared a space. In college we'd learned a skill known as brainstorming. It involves a clean sheet of paper, a pencil, and every random idea that pops into your head. Exploring all sorts of possibilities could lead to a problem's unexpected solution, the professors told us. A good theory, I decided now, grinding a pencil in the sharpener until it glistened with a point that looked lethal. I blew off the shavings that clung to it and tapped the tip against my blank paper. I let the "what if?" question tumble around in my head for a few moments and then, feeling a little foolish, scribbled down the stream of my meandering thoughts.

Inside of five minutes I'd produced about a dozen answers to my question. They ranged from possible to probable to ludicrous. But only one kept leaping off the page at me and waving a banner.

It read: *What if Roland and Janet were an item?*

The words on the paper blurred as my eyes stared vacantly ahead, following the path of this idea. In the library all was still. Somewhere in the room, a clock ticked off the minutes in a steady, solemn fashion, providing rhythm to the rain still pouring down outside.

Very deliberately I picked up the pencil

and made a checkmark in the margin of my paper. Here, I was certain, was the solution to my mystery. All I had to do was piece it together so it made sense. A tall order. I tried to be rational and logical and calm, but it seemed that, once started, brainstorming was hard to control.

Chances are, I told myself sternly, *I'm way off the mark on this. But just suppose. . .*

In no time I'd sent the pencil scratching over the paper again, making notes of further explanation. My hand moved quickly across the page, leaving behind a smudgy, barely legible trail of ideas. Each premise led to another, and I couldn't help but wonder if my imagination was coloring events to fit my own hypothesis.

As I fitted the pieces into place, turning them this way and that, my excitement mounted. Several times I had to leap from my chair to pace up and down the library stacks, ridding myself of nervous energy. Briskly I marched up one aisle and down the next, mumbling aloud and poking the air with the end of my pencil for emphasis. Anyone happening upon me would have been certain I was suffering from delusion.

And, right about then, I might have agreed with them.

Chapter Fourteen

The more I examined the situation, playing devil's advocate and debating every point, the more I became convinced.

Returning to my desk, I wished desperately for a soda. My throat felt parched, my lips dry and warm. The rain was sliding down the windows in smooth, thick sheets, and that old song about "cool, clear water" popped into my head as I watched. Still, it was unthinkable to stop now. Wandering away was impossible.

I gripped my pencil firmly between my hands, spinning it around and feeling its smooth surface glide across my fingers.

Roland's diary made it pretty clear he was besotted with Janet. Janet had always had nothing but wonderful things to say about Roland. An illicit love affair, however brief. . . .

My heart was pounding now in anticipation and dread. Following this line of reasoning was frightening, but follow it I must.

A brief flash of lightning lit the room, then came a crescendo of thunder. The sound was coming from all around me, echoing on, lasting a lifetime. It rumbled beneath my feet, shaking the walls, rattling the glass of the big windows. I jumped, the pencil in my hand snapping as my body jerked from the chair. I spun around, half expecting to see the windows broken and walls of water pouring forth.

The storm continued, unabated, but no damage had been done. The heavy panes of glass kept the wild, uncontrolled force safely away from me.

I felt as if other dangerous forces had also been unleashed, however. It took several moments of deep and even breathing for me to regain a semblance of calm, but even that was only on the surface. Turmoil and triumph battled within me. My triumph at filling in the blanks was overwhelmed by turmoil as the full realization of this answer dawned.

For if there had been a child, that child would legally be a Peabody.

Hurriedly I cast aside the broken halves of my pencil and reached into my pocket for another. Paper crackled beneath my fingers, and I remembered the yellowed scrap that had fallen from Roland's diary. My curiosity boundless now, I pulled it out and eased the brittle creases open. I had been expecting another newspaper clipping. I was wrong. The letter said:

Dear Roland,

Thank you so much for the lovely gifts for the baby. He's a sweet little thing, and the nurses say he sleeps like an angel. I can't wait to see you! Please come with Frank as soon as you can. He has been very understanding about all this, although we both have always realized how indebted we are to you. Now, with little Johnny, we are truly one big happy family!

Your loving Janet

Well, this was food for thought! Janet's eagerness to see Roland seemed to lend weight to my growing theory, as did her remark about being a family. My mind drifted as I drummed my pencil on the blotter.

"*Indebted,*" she'd written. That must refer to Frank and that long-ago burglary, I deduced. It almost seemed as though Frank were blackmailed — powerless to ever speak up. That made it easier to understand his sullen expression and defeated, angry attitude.

Blinking, I ended the trancelike state I'd entered, my eyes focusing reluctantly on the room before me. Mentally giving myself a shake, I tried to remember that all my conclusions were still mere suppositions. I had been literally reading between the lines. Until this time, I'd been doing my plotting without a thought of what my next step would be. Now my fondest wish was to find Richard. Telling him the story and sharing my theory would make it real.

It would also open me up for plenty of trouble if I turned out to be wrong. I squared my shoulders. I was right. I knew it. Beyond a doubt. All I needed was confirmation and that. . . . Well, that would have to come from Janet.

I did a few more laps around the library. Pinching my eyes shut, I tried to picture Janet and the man who would be Johnny, hoping to see a family resemblance. Both Janet and Andrew had the same jawline, but beyond that I couldn't think of any similarities.

The mind is a funny and wonderful thing. It does some work for us, on occasion, taking bits of seemingly unrelated information and turning them into coherent thought. That's what happened now, with the force of a thunderclap.

The vision in my mind was Andrew on the day of our bike ride. Standing on the shore of the cove, he looked out over the lake. On his forehead, in bold relief, was a small, crescent-shaped scar.

"It was a difficult birth," Janet had told me. *"They'd had to use forceps."*

I bit my lip. Having no idea what a forceps scar would look like, this was flimsy evidence, indeed. Still, it could be the proof I needed. Before I could lose my nerve, I was out the door of the library and headed for Janet's domain — the kitchen. The trip seemed especially long now as I moved swiftly down the hall, trying not to break into a trot. My excitement was barely held in check.

I must confess, I had no thoughts of danger. I didn't expect any. After all, to the best of my knowledge, I'd just be rattling a few skeletons in the Peabody closet. I'd let Andrew deal with the matter of the vanishing books when he brought in the police.

The gentle sound of humming came from the direction of the kitchen, accompanied by the familiar clatter and tink of dishes being moved around. Janet at work. The hammering of my heart slowed, and a heavy, dull feeling similar to pain took its place. My mouth felt cottony and dry, thick with anxiety. But I'd come too far to stop now.

The kitchen door opened with a slight

squeak of hinges, and Janet looked up from her work at the countertop. The look of curiosity dropped from her face and was replaced by a hesitant smile.

"Hello, Sarah," she said, looking down at her hands, busily kneading dough.

When she glanced back up, I still stood in silence near the big wooden table. She frowned quizzically, one gray eyebrow shooting up. I swallowed, suddenly at a loss for words.

"What is it now, Sarah?" she asked, not unkindly. "Now what must you know?"

Thank you, I thought, *for giving me an opening.* Taking a deep breath I felt all the way down to my toes, I opened my mouth. "When Johnny was born, did the forceps leave a scar?" The words were bald and shocking, as I'd meant them to be.

Janet's reaction was just what I was expecting. I watched her closely, saw her face blanch. Several emotions passed quickly across her features — surprise, fear, and then, feigned ignorance. Her hands stopped their automatic motion and were still, buried up to the knuckles in soft, white dough.

"I — I —" She broke off, clearing her throat and avoiding my eyes. "Why do you ask?"

Running my finger absently around the

ridge on the end of the table, I said, "I think you know why. I did as you asked and trusted you. Janet, I drew the only conclusion there is."

For a long moment we looked at each other across the wide expanse of the room. Then Janet nodded, her shoulders bowed in defeat. The lines in her face seemed to deepen, and the sparkle of sudden tears filmed her eyes.

"Am I right, Janet? Your son didn't drown in the lake. Roland Clayton's nephew did. Andrew is dead and Johnny is alive. Johnny — your son. And Roland's son."

She pressed her eyes tightly shut, sending fine lines dancing across her cheeks. "Yes," she whispered. "Yes, that's it. Our boy is alive."

Here it was, the confirmation I needed. But instead of feeling excited, I felt startled, as if I'd never really expected this twisted story to be true. I stepped closer to her.

"Why, Janet? Why did you let Roland turn Johnny into Andrew? How could you abandon your own son?"

"I never abandoned him!" Her eyes flew open, their glisten gone in an instant. "I was always here for him. Always!"

"But you couldn't call him yours. You let Roland claim him."

218

"I had to, Sarah! I had no choice. He did it all so quickly. By the time I realized, it was too late to change. I would have been calling him a liar, and it would still just be my word against his."

"How did it happen?" I pressed.

She shrugged briefly. "Just after . . . the accident, Frank and I took Johnny back to the house. To get him warm and make sure he was all right. Roland went immediately to the mainland, to fetch the doctor for Johnny and report what had happened to the authorities. He brought back a rescue team, and they poked around in the water for a while, but, of course, it was too late."

She paused in her narrative to look up at me. "You have to understand how it was, Sarah. I was in shock. We all were. When the doctor arrived to examine Johnny, calling him Andrew, I'm not sure I even heard him. It wasn't until later, after everyone had gone, that Roland told me what he had done." She clamped her lips together, her hands tightly fisted in her lap. "He said he did it for me and for Johnny. He said it was for the best."

"Did what, Janet? What did Roland do?"

When she spoke, her anger made her voice shake. "He told them it was Johnny

219

who died. He told them we saved Andrew and lost Johnny."

I thought I could see the way Roland's mind was working, what he hoped to do by his action, but I asked, anyway. "Why did he do that? What did he hope to gain?"

Janet gave a laugh without humor. "Well, just what he got! He turned his illegitimate son into his very legitimate nephew. In the eyes of the law, my Johnny was now Roland's heir. It was an awful thing to do to me. To us." She spread her hands. "But it was so easy. We're very isolated here. No one really knew either of the boys, and they looked similar. Had the same color hair and eyes. It was taken as fact on the mainland. The death certificate went on record."

"And that was that."

Janet gave a little sigh, her breath coming out in a long quiver. "Yes. That was that. I couldn't change it. Roland was a very powerful man. No one would have believed me. And . . . and, well, we owed Roland a lot. He saved us from —" She stopped and would not go on.

"I know about Frank and the ivory theft, Janet. It was in Roland's diary," I said.

She nodded. "But there were circumstances you don't know, Sarah. Not that it makes burglary acceptable," she hastened to add. "Just, maybe, understandable." She looked up at me, and our eyes met as she continued. "I'd been very ill, in the hospital. For a while they didn't think I'd live. By the time I had recovered, the doctor bills were astronomical. We were young — just starting out — and we didn't have any money. Frank had done some work at the Hamilton estate and knew about the ivory collection. He told me what he had in mind, and I begged him not to even consider it." She pounded the palms of her hands together. "I told him not to do it! Said we'd find the money. Somewhere! But the next thing I knew, Frank had a bullet in his leg and was being carried into our house by a man I'd never seen before. The man was Roland Clayton."

"Why didn't Roland call the police and turn Frank in?" I asked.

"Because he wanted the ivory for himself. I guess collectors aren't always scrupulous. He knew it was stolen; he knew Frank was in trouble. He offered us a way out from under our problems."

"By coming to Echo Moon?" I guessed.

"Yes. Roland gave us the money for the hospital bills. It was a mere pittance to him — just a fraction of what the ivory was worth. In return, we came here, forever in his debt.

And he kept his friend's precious netsuke." Her voice was heavy, sharp with bitterness as she recounted the details of the episode that had changed her life in so many ways.

"Andrew told me —" I began and broke off. I shook my head. "I can't help thinking of him as Andrew."

Janet's lips turned up in a brief smile. "I always do too. After all these years. What did he tell you?"

Thinking back over the weeks, I recalled our first conversation. "He said you were like a mother to him."

Again, that trace of smile crossed Janet's features. "I've done my best," she said, not without some pride.

I tried to imagine what the years must have been like for her, never able to call her son her own, sharing him with the wealthy bachelor she loved and yet wouldn't allow herself to have. It was hard to doubt her motivations. She seemed so sincere, almost innocent. She couldn't be guilty of anything but caring too much. Could she?

Across the room, Janet began to push and pull at the dough before her. I pulled out one of the heavy wooden chairs and sat down.

"He had a better life, didn't he?" I asked, elaborating when Janet glanced up at me questioningly. "As the nephew of a wealthy man he had every luxury. A wonderful position in life, the best education, clothes, travel." I ticked the items off on my fingers, but Janet was already shaking her head.

"No," she said. "I know what you're thinking, and you're wrong."

Again.

"It's true that as Andrew Clayton he got things he couldn't have gotten otherwise. He did have all those advantages you said, but that wasn't what I ever wanted." She held out her hands in appeal, floury palms facing up to the ceiling. "Do you think I would have chosen to live this lie? It was dishonest and deceitful. But Roland was in control." Her frail shoulders lifted; then she firmly punched one fist into the dough, and I wondered if she wished it were me. "He said no one would be hurt. Except Frank. Except me. But I didn't really lose my son," she tried to convince us both. "I . . . I shared him."

I shut my eyes, grimacing, unable to follow this crazy form of logic. Despite myself, however, I could almost understand. If I were Janet, I might have reacted in the same fashion. Out of fear, or loyalty, or love, would I have relinquished my claim to my child? It's easy to answer questions that are only hypothetical. Answering the genuine ones is much trickier. I tried not to be judgmental, but it wasn't easy.

"Does he know?" I asked. "Does Andrew have any idea what happened?"

Abruptly Janet's hands stopped moving, and I wondered fleetingly if this pie would ever see the oven. "No!" she nearly shouted. "He doesn't know. We've never told him. Oh, Sarah, promise you won't tell him! Promise me!" Her eyes were wide with panic, and hastened to reassure her. The very thought of spilling these decades-old beans was unsettling. It was not a job I would ever volunteer for, that was certain.

"That is the furthest thing from my mind," I confessed. "The truth must come from you and Frank."

"It's too late now. He'd never understand." Her rising voice echoed the anxiety written on her features. She'd folded her hands into her apron, wringing them fiercely.

"Well, that's your decision to make," I said, escaping the responsibility. I had another question that needed asking now, one I'd put off for too long already.

"Janet, someone has been stealing books from Mr. Clayton's library and selling them. I have a good reason to suspect Frank."

Pausing, I saw disbelief on Janet's face. She opened and closed her mouth several times without saying a word. I went on. "Why would he steal from his boss?"

Slowly, the corners of Janet's mouth drew down, and her eyes went dull and lifeless. She abandoned her project and walked painfully over to the table, tugging mightily at one of the heavy chairs before slumping into it. The big chair seemed to swallow her up as she rubbed the heels of her hands against her eyes.

"Stolen books? Frank?" she asked in a quiet, tired voice. "Sarah, I don't understand." Looking up at me, her eyes pleaded for an explanation.

I did my best to provide it. Actually, there weren't many facts to convey, no story to elaborate on, no convoluted machinations. Explaining about the missing books took just a few moments. Bringing in Emil and his detective work tracking the books to their source took a bit longer.

Throughout, Janet continued to shake her head in disbelief. "Not Frank. Not Frank," she repeated as each new wrinkle unfolded. "That's all behind us."

"I can bring you the letter from Emil if you like," I offered. "It makes things pretty clear."

"But why?" Janet wailed, taking me by surprise. "We don't need money. We've always been happy here. Why would Frank do such a thing?" Breaking down entirely, she buried her face in her hands and wept.

As she shook with each sob, I circled the table and came to stand behind her. Placing my hands on her shoulders, I said, "I'm sorry, Janet. I don't know why he did it, either."

"I have to see him. I have to ask him. Right now!" She straightened up, strong again and ready to fight. "Frank will be able to explain all this. He'll clear it up in a minute. You'll see." Struggling to her feet, she asked, "Where is he?"

The hinges of the kitchen door squeaked, and both our heads turned in that direction. "Where is who?" Frank asked in his gruff, surly tone. He seemed to fill the doorway, his eyes black and angry. His face was unreadable, as always.

When he moved farther into the room, I could see Andrew behind him.

Chapter Fifteen

Janet and I stood in a stunned silence, looking at the two of them as if they were ghosts. My heart had resumed its double-time pace, and I had to cling tightly to the back of the chair to keep from falling over. My knees were shaking, sending jolts of fear and adrenaline through my body.

The classic showdown scene faced me, and I wasn't sure I could handle it. I wasn't ready. I needed support. Oh, where was Richard, anyhow?

"Oh, Frank," Janet said with a little cry of distress. "She says you're stealing things!" Janet's heavy-heeled shoes clunked against the floor as she deserted me to run to her husband's side.

I stood alone, facing the three of them and their looks of anger and suspicion. My grip on the chair faltered. My palms were sweaty, and I dropped my hands to my sides.

My worst nightmare come true! Alone and accused before sullen Frank Peabody and the ever more confounding "Andrew

Clayton." Frank's arm went around Janet's shoulder in a protective gesture I would have found touching at any other time. He looked from her to me, and he didn't look happy. When I glanced at Andrew, I was stunned to see a half smile on his face, as if he were enjoying the little drama unfolding before him.

"Tell her she's wrong, Frank," Janet pleaded in pathetic tones. Her small hand clutched at his shirtfront, and she refused to look at me.

"What have you been saying?" he asked, the heat of his glare jumping the short distance across the table to where I stood.

Well, I couldn't lie, because Janet was there to confirm or deny my remarks. And besides, a part of me (a very small part) was ready for a showdown. The deceptions had gone on long enough. My hands sought the chair back again for support. I swallowed hard and straightened my spine. Addressing Andrew, I said, "The missing books I told you about have been traced. They were sold in South Clifton by a man calling himself Pete Johnson. His description fits Frank."

The smile dropped from Andrew's lips, replaced by a look of mock amazement. "Frank, is this true?" He drew out the sentence, turning it into a joke, laughing at me.

I bristled but said nothing. Frank, too, made no remark. His lips pressed firmly together spoke of anger barely held in check.

"Well?" Andrew prodded, leaning over to thrust his face into Frank's, nose to nose.

Frank backed away, saying, "You know full well what's been happening. Was your idea."

Janet's head lifted abruptly, and I took a step nearer the dangerous group, not trusting my ears.

"Your idea?" Janet echoed, looking from one to the other as if she'd never seen them before. "What do you mean? What's this all about?"

It seemed I'd been forgotten entirely. I used this stolen time to assess my surroundings. The people across the room blocked the door to the dining room, but the back door of the house was just through the passage to my left. If I had to, and if I could move quickly enough, there would be a way out of the house. And into the storm.

"Answer me!" Frank barked and I jumped. I hadn't heard his question.

"I'm sorry," I said stupidly. "What did you say?"

"He said, 'Tell us what you think you know,'" Andrew broke in, leaving the Peabodys' side to range nervously back and forth across the kitchen. When he got close to me, he reached a hand out toward my shoulder, as if to touch me. I closed my eyes, flinching at the gesture, and he abruptly dropped his arm and stepped away.

This time when I answered, I spoke to Frank. "I know the books are gone. I know you stole them. I know. . . ." Here I faltered for an instant, choosing my words with care. "I know what happened on the ice all those years ago. I know the truth."

"Is that truth with a capital T?" Andrew asked sarcastically, laughing in a high-pitched, grating way.

"Shut up!" Frank snapped, his voice vicious. He thrust Janet behind him, out of harm's way. The two men squared off like boxers before a fight. The air seemed charged with their anger and with the energy of the storm outside. I tried to edge nearer the passage leading from the room as Frank and Andrew circled each other in the middle.

"She knows," Frank said in a menacing way. "What do you plan to do now? I told you it was stupid to bring strangers in. You should have listened to me."

"Listen to you? I had to bring people in — to satisfy the lawyers for the estate, you fool! I'd never have done it otherwise. If I'd listened to you, I'd be stuck on this island forever!" Andrew spat.

"But you'd be safe!" Frank retorted.

"Safe?" Andrew's tone was incredulous. "Why would I want to be safe if it meant being here the rest of my life? You may be crazy, but I'm not."

"Don't you talk that way!" Janet jumped in, wagging a finger as if the angry young man before her were an errant child. "You've no right to say such things. You don't understand."

"I understand plenty!" Andrew's eyes focused pointedly on Frank, and there was a heavy, pregnant pause before he went on, shifting his gaze to Janet. "Mother dear." He turned the title into a sneer, as if hoping to cause Frank pain.

Janet and I both gave a gasp. I looked anxiously at her, but she did not see me. She held one hand against her throat and used the other to steady herself against the table.

I remained where I was, watching in fascination and shock. I had wondered if Andrew knew what I referred to when I mentioned the ice to Frank. Now I had my answer. He, too, knew the truth. How had he found out? When did he realize?

"You imbecile!" Frank made a grab for

Andrew's arm, but the younger man avoided him easily, dancing out of reach.

"How did he know?" Janet asked of no one in particular. Dejected, she kept her glance down and repeated, "How?"

"Shall I tell her, Frank, or will you?" Andrew goaded. He had maneuvered over to the sink now, so we were positioned like the points of a triangle, with Frank and Janet directly across from me, and Andrew on the opposite wall.

Frank remained silent, glaring at Andrew, who merely grinned before continuing. "It isn't easy to publicly admit you've been made a cuckold, hmm? Well, if it helps you any, Frank, it wasn't easy for Uncle to tell me, either. But just before the end, when he knew he was dying, that's what he did. He made me promise to keep his secret till my dying day. Then" — his voice dropped to a whisper, turning soft and gentle — "then he told me of the love of his life. He told me about the woman he had always cherished and adored and how he longed to make her his wife, but could not, because she was already married to another."

As he spoke, I watched the Peabodys clinging to each other across the room. Tortured Frank, blackmailed about his past, seeing the woman he loved grow to love

232

another and yet retain her loyalty to him. Sad-eyed Janet, loving two men, unwilling to give up either, suffering throughout her life from the consequences of her indecision.

"He told me they had had a child. That I was that child. He told me Janet was his true love."

At this, Janet put her face in her hands, hiding her tears. Was she crying over what was or what might have been?

"I promised to continue my unwitting masquerade and act the role of nephew as if I were none the wiser." He looked up, right at me. "But I was wiser, and I saw my way out. I started to liquidate."

"And everything would have been fine if it weren't for these strangers," Frank growled suddenly, looking over at me as if I were to blame for all this. "I warned you to stay away!" he said to me. "I left that note in your room. But, no, you didn't listen. You ruined everything!"

Stunned into silence, I remained motionless.

"Well, how was I to know dear Uncle Roland made an inventory?" Andrew asked. "It would have worked out if it weren't for that. I'd have this place fixed up to satisfy Uncle's requirements, but I'd also have a little money on the side from all those books no one will ever read, anyhow." Andrew's voice was so matter-of-fact when he spoke, making those facts clear to us all.

"You made Frank sell those books!" Janet accused her son. "You made Frank do it, didn't you?" Frank's grip on her shoulders tightened, holding her against him when she would have charged at the younger man.

"I had no choice, Janet," Frank said. "He knew about the ivory scam from all those years ago. Roland must have told him. So Andrew could threaten me just as Roland always had. He said he'd go to the cops and turn me in. I'd be sent away. Probably for the rest of my life."

"No!" Janet's cry was like that of a wounded creature. She snapped her eyes over to Andrew, who was leaning casually against a countertop. Her hurt and anger were clearly visible.

Andrew sighed, as if he were becoming bored with the discussion. "Yes, yes. I did say I'd do that. And I still will, if I have to."

"But after all this time who would believe you?" Janet asked.

With a shrug and another malicious smile, Andrew said, "Why wouldn't the police believe me? It's the truth. So, you see, old Frank here had no options. It was play along or go to jail."

"But why did you sell the books? And the paintings?" I asked. "You must have inherited plenty of money as Roland's nephew. It couldn't have been for that."

In a slow and deliberate motion, Andrew picked up a paring knife from the counter and ran the point of it under each of his fingernails as he explained. "Dear Uncle — I suppose I should really call him Dad or Father or Pops, but I think I'll stick to Uncle — well, he had this work-ethic hangup, which was awfully amusing in a man born into a wealthy family. He left me the estate and just enough money to keep it running each year. Sort of like an allowance." He wrinkled his nose in distaste, and when he spoke again, his voice was cold with fury. "He actually said if I wanted more money than the pittance he left me, I'd have to earn it on my own! That was why he made me start that stupid realty business. He was setting me up!"

I swallowed and bravely said, "So you figured you could take whatever you could get your hands on before it became part of the legal inventory and turn it into cash. Sell the Clayton collection bit by bit before it was recorded — before anyone would notice it was missing."

"That's right." Andrew looked at the Peabodys. "And a wonderful plan it was." Turning to me, he went on. "Of course, now that you know, everything has changed. I could force these two to clam up, but you. . . ." His eyebrows creased in thought, the knife still held in one hand. "You won't be such an easy problem to solve."

My heart beat so rapidly, I was certain the sound of it filled the room. I said unconvincingly, "I won't tell. I promise!"

Andrew laughed again, shaking his head slowly from side to side. "Should I believe you?" he asked, stepping closer. "I don't. You're too honest by half. I must say your concern over the insurance on the library was touching. I'm sure it will please you to know I've filed claims with the company and plan to report this horrible burglary to the police." He clucked his tongue. "Tsk, tsk. Such a tragedy," he went on. "People will be saying Echo Moon is cursed."

"Cursed?" Janet repeated. "It isn't. You know it isn't!"

Again Andrew shrugged, cocking his head to one side. "I'm not so sure," he drawled. "The drowning all those years ago. Then a burglary. Then another death." He slid his gaze over at me, and my blood turned to ice in my veins.

"What are you saying?" My voice was no more than a whisper. Even I could hear the quiver in it.

"I'm sorry, Sarah. Truly." Andrew came to my side, backing me into the corner without touching me. His face looked sunburned — red and shiny, except where the scar was, half hidden beneath a tousled lock of hair. "I had plans for us, you know. Mr. and Mrs. Andrew Clayton. Doesn't that sound nice?"

I shook my head, not wanting to hear any more. Leaning to one side, I tried to catch the eye of Frank or Janet, but they remained across the room, focused on this madman.

"Doesn't it?" Andrew's hands grabbed my shoulders, giving me a violent shake. My head banged against the wall, and tears sprang to my eyes. I blinked them away.

"I'd never marry you. I don't love you."

"That wouldn't have mattered. I always get what I want, and I wanted you. But not any more."

"F-f-fine, then. I'll leave just as soon as the rain stops," I said. Reaching up, I whisked my bangs back from my forehead nervously.

Andrew's hand closed on mine as I did,

his grasp firm and painful. "No," he hissed. "You'll leave now. With me." He began to walk toward the door, pulling me along. With my other hand I grabbed at the table, the chair, the doorjamb. My feet stumbled reluctantly over each other, and I looked to the Peabodys for help.

"Stop him!" I shouted. "He's going to kill me!" I knew as certainly as I knew my own name that the death Andrew referred to would be my own.

Frank stood rigid, as if turned to stone. The crisis point had left him paralyzed. I knew he would take no action. We were near the doorway when Janet intervened, pulling free of Frank's grasp and dashing across the room to hang onto Andrew's arm.

"Don't! Don't do this! Sarah won't tell anyone what's happened. No one will ever know if you let her go now," she pleaded.

Andrew stopped. He looked into his mother's face and, for a moment, his expression softened. I held my breath, wondering if Janet's appeal would touch him.

Tenderly he reached out, placing his hand against her wrinkled cheek. "I'll be all right, Ma," he said gently, reassuring her. "I'll be safe and she'll be gone." His grip on my wrist ached, but I knew better than to try to pull away.

"No, Johnny, no." Tears had come to Janet's eyes and spilled over as I watched. She shook her head, chin trembling, and repeated her plea. But Andrew was adamant.

"It'll be okay. You'll see." With startling speed he leaned over to drop a kiss on his mother's brow. Then, without looking at me, he started out the door, pulling me behind him like an unwieldy parcel.

"Call the police!" I shouted to Janet just before the back door closed behind us. I couldn't be sure if she had heard me. Andrew had, however.

As we set off into the rain, Andrew laughed and said, "Even if they do call the cops, it'll be too late by the time they get here from the mainland. You think you're so smart. I'd have thought you'd know that."

Our feet slipped on the wet grass as he started in the direction of the dock. The rain fell heavy and steady, making it difficult to see, soaking us in no time at all. I could only hope the delays would last long enough for help to come and sent up prayers that Richard and his men would appear from behind the next tree. Andrew didn't stick to the gravel road I had traveled so frequently, but cut a path instead through the woods.

With the gray sky overhead and the shadow from the trees, the woods were as dark as nightfall. Unseen branches snatched at my arms and face. Brambles from bushes scratched at my legs. The mud underfoot pulled at my feet. And still, the madman with me plunged on, cursing my slowness, yanking me brutally to my feet when I stumbled and fell.

Once, it was he who lost his balance, tripping over an exposed tree root, sprawling headlong on the forest floor. Stunned to be suddenly free of his grasp, I lost several seconds deciding which path to follow before taking flight. As Andrew pulled himself from the mud, I veered left and ran.

Holding my arms before my face to ward off low-hanging branches, I pushed through the dense foliage as quickly as possible, hoping to lose myself in their camouflage. Like a rabbit fleeing a hunter, I moved rapidly, my heart pounding with fear. I couldn't stop to think about the situation, or I'd be paralyzed with terror, so I let the instinct for self-preservation take over.

Raindrops slid down my face like the tears I didn't have time to cry. Hastily I wiped them away and tried to discern where I was and, more importantly, where Andrew was.

I leaned wearily up against an oak tree,

its gnarly bark rough behind my fingers. Gasping for breath, I strained my ears, listening for sounds from the underbrush. Only the gentle hiss of the rain could be heard, mixing with the song of the wind through the trees. For several moments I remained there, motionless and silent, before I felt safe enough to draw a deep breath. Looking around me, into the thick of the dark woods, I realized I was well and truly lost. One direction looked exactly like another. I had no idea where I was or which way would lead me back to the house and the relative safety I could find there.

When my heartbeat had slowed to something like normal, I tried to think, but wilderness survival was foreign to me, especially without the sun to indicate direction. Maybe, I thought, I'd just stay right here. Until help found me. But what if he found me first? That idea was enough to spur me into motion. Any action was better than inaction.

I turned right, only because the ground seemed to climb there, and I knew I must go uphill to reach the house. I tried to move quietly, stealthily, but by now I was tired and frightened and miserable. Perhaps that made me careless. I only know that one moment I was alone in the woods, pushing my way forward, and the next, he was there.

Out of the shadows he leaped in front of me. Covered in mud, with blood from several scratches staining one cheek, he was a terrifying sight. My body went cold all over, but my heart pounding in my ears proved I hadn't died from the shock. My shriek split the air for just an instant as I wheeled to run. Andrew grabbed at my arm, but I pulled away. When he launched his body at me like a missile, I had no time to move. He crashed into my back, slamming me facedown onto the forest floor. All the breath went out of me in a whoosh and we were both still.

I could feel tree roots and twigs and stones pressing into my skin and wondered if I'd broken any bones in the fall. Andrew kept me pinned there, twisting both hands into my hair, pulling it till the tears smarted in my eyes. Leaning over, he hissed in my ear, "You'd make a rotten Girl Scout. You walked in a circle!" His maniacal laughter echoed through the forest, ringing in my ears and taunting me.

He slid his hands from my hair to my throat and tightened them. It was difficult enough to breathe with my nose pressed against the ground and his heavy weight on my back. Now I gasped, flailing my arms and legs, struggling for air.

"I could kill you now," he said, his fingers digging into the flesh of my neck, "but it wouldn't look much like an accident. So we're going down to the dock, and you're going to walk directly in front of me, with no more valiant escape attempts. Do you understand?"

I tried to nod but couldn't. Swallowing, I said hoarsely, "Yes."

"Good." His weight eased off me as he stood, and my hands went instantly to my injured throat. Sitting up, I was able to breathe deeply, but the breaths were ragged as the sobs I could no longer contain shook my body. The situation seemed hopeless. No way to escape and no help in sight. But I wasn't ready to die. Not when love had found me and I had everything to live for. I struggled to my feet and marched silently before my captor, my brain working furiously all the while. If another opportunity presented itself, I'd try again to get away.

We were nearing the shore now, I could tell. Above the sound of the rain was the rush of the waves. As we burst through the last stand of trees and emerged on the gravel near the dock, my eyes took in the storm-ravaged lake. The sky hung low and gray over the water; the clouds looked ready to sink into the waves. The water was nearly black and seemed to be boiling, churning under the wind and tossing up whitecaps that scudded onto shore with a deafening crash.

My feet stopped of their own accord, refusing to move closer to those raging depths. Andrew's poke in the small of my back made me stumble a few steps forward, and I turned to face him, ready to plead for my life.

"Please," I begged, holding both hands out imploringly.

Closing his hand tightly over my wrist, Andrew cursed and I followed his gaze out over the water, wondering what he had seen. And then I saw it too.

Far out, just off the horizon, a light beamed between the rise and fall of the waves. A boat, braving the storm, was headed our way. The police!

My heart leaped inside me, and for the first time in a long while I allowed myself to hope. Waving the arm Andrew didn't hold, I jumped up and down, shouting above the storm. Logic told me my words would never reach that far-off boat, but I had to try.

"Quiet!" Andrew shouted, twisting my other arm behind me. "Shut up! Shut up!"

His voice was high and raspy. He was losing control, and he knew it.

He turned his head frantically from side to side, stopping when he caught sight of Richard's pathetic little rowboat, bobbing like a toy at the side of the pier. "C'mon!" he ordered.

Half dragging me behind him, he ran across the short distance separating us from the boat. I did all I could to delay our steps, digging in my heels and sitting down on the sharp pebbles. Andrew didn't even seem to notice, he was so intent on his objective. He just hauled me along over the stones until I scrambled to my feet once more.

"We'll have to hurry! Hurry! Hurry!" he was saying to himself, like a chant. Our pounding feet hit the wooden planks of the pier, and they sagged beneath us.

I hesitated again at the water's edge. The wind was much stronger here on the lake and whipped my hair around my head, into my eyes and my mouth. Impatiently I shoved it away. Looking out across the water, I could see that the light among the waves had grown brighter and bigger. The ship was getting closer! I had to hang on, with help so nearby.

"Get in!" Andrew shouted from behind me, giving me another push. "Get in the boat!" I jerked away from his touch, stepping back from him and the tiny vessel he intended me to die in.

"Get in now!" Andrew came at me with the force of ten. His arms grasped my shoulders so fiercely the pain made me gasp. Then my feet left the pier and I was falling, hurled into the front of the boat.

With a bone-jarring crash, I landed half on the seat and half off. I remember striking my head on the metal side of the craft, and then the world went black.

Chapter Sixteen

It couldn't have been more than two or three minutes before I regained consciousness. When my eyes opened, the first thing I saw was the black and angry sky above. I had slid to the floor of the boat, apparently, and was staring straight up. My head pounded, pulsing with my heartbeat, and I was afraid to move, knowing movement would increase the pain.

There was a horrendous buzzing filling my ears, drilling into my brain. It took me several seconds to identify it as the outboard motor. We were on the lake now, bucking the huge waves caused by the storm. Out of the corner of my eye, I could see Andrew at the back of the boat. With one hand on the motor and his face set in grim determination, he steered the tiny craft out . . . out . . . . out. How much farther did he intend to go? I wondered. How much closer to the ever-approaching ship I was sure contained the police?

He must have felt my eyes on him because just then he looked over. His brow furrowed in a scowl, he shouted above the cacophony, "You should do as you're told. Then you wouldn't get hurt."

Ludicrous words from a man planning to kill me. The remark was all I needed to send me over the edge of hysteria. A bubble of laughter caught in my throat and, opening wide, I let it out, laughing till the tears ran down my face to mix with the rain.

Andrew's face darkened, turning hard and expressionless. Abruptly he stopped the boat's motor. Without its whining sound buzzing around us, it was easier to hear the slap of the water against the side of the boat, the rush of the waves tumbling under the wind.

My moment of madness died in terror as I looked first at the angry, inky darkness of the water, then at Andrew's frightening countenance. The only other vessel out on the lake was so close now, I could see its outline. In an instant I was able to recognize it. Bravely confronting the storm, the *Molly Jane* lumbered ever closer. Could it reach me in time?

Even as I thought the question, Andrew stood up in the tiny boat, bracing his legs as it rolled from side to side. I clutched the seat with both hands, cowering under his stare, and scrambled into the farthest corner until there was nowhere else to go. Just a foot beyond, the water rose and fell as if it were alive and waiting impatiently to snap me in its jaws.

"Good-bye, Miss Holmes," Andrew sneered, reaching onto the floor of the boat and hoisting one of the oars effortlessly. He swung the heavy wooden tool onto his shoulder like a baseball bat, then held it aloft. "Sorry I can't say it's been nice knowing you."

I saw his shoulder begin to shift backward in preparation for the blow that would kill me. The weight of the oar was behind him, out over the water, as the boat continued to pitch and roll in the storm.

It was now or never.

In a flash I lunged to one side, throwing all my weight against the boat. It dipped down sharply. The water rushed in, cold and startling. With clenched hands I held on as we bobbed in the opposite direction. The sudden motion caught Andrew off balance, as I'd hoped it would. He stumbled, shifting his feet on the wet, slick bottom, but the awkward paddle poised near his shoulder carried him over. For an instant a look of surprise crossed his face. His eyes widened, and his mouth gaped open. With a scream he hit the water and was immediately lost beneath the surface.

I watched in shock for a moment, my fingers still clutching the boat as the water swirled around my feet. The oar bobbed with the waves about ten feet off, but Andrew did not reappear. My nerves were in tatters when the lights of the *Molly Jane* found me. I shielded my eyes and stared up at the men crowded against the railing. Captain Bill and my darling Richard stood next to a man in a police uniform.

Richard's face glowed white with worry, his brow creased and his lips pressed into a hard, thin line. Our eyes met across the water. "Are you all right?" he shouted through cupped hands.

Slumped on the seat of the rowboat, I nodded, then yelled, "Andrew went over. He's . . . he's. . . ." I pointed at the spot where he had disappeared, shaking my head and babbling incoherently.

"We're coming! We're coming!" Richard hollered. "Don't move, Sarah. We'll be right there."

Chuck and Joe lowered a rope ladder over the edge of the ship as it came up alongside the rowboat. It took the last of my courage to cling to the prickly, damp rungs and suspend myself over the churning water. Holding my breath, I climbed up, encouraged by Richard's reassuring voice. Soon his arms were around my shoulders, helping to pull me over the edge of the ship, onto the safety of the deck and into the haven of his arms.

Hours later a hastily dispatched Coast Guard ship continued searching for Andrew's body. Darkness had long since fallen, and even though the storm had passed and the rain had ended, the rescuers were having a difficult time.

After the authorities had arrived on the scene, the *Molly Jane* had proceeded to the island. Now I sat in the seldom-used drawing room, my hands folded around a steaming cup of coffee. Richard was beside me, his arm along the back of the sofa, his hand caressing my shoulder. I had finally stopped trembling and could look around the room without shuddering at the thought of what had happened in this house earlier.

Richard had listened in silence to my recounting of the day's events, even though he'd already heard the story when I told it all to the police. Shaking his head in disbelief, he said, "I still can't believe John Peabody masqueraded as Andrew Clayton all those years. Good detective work on your part, Sarah — or should I say Sherlock? — Holmes." Leaning over, he kissed my cheek tenderly and gave me an abbreviated bear hug. "I'm so glad you're safe. I don't know what I would have done if we'd come too late." His voice broke off with a catch at the end.

When I glanced at him, I was touched to see the glimmer of tears in his eyes. "Well, you weren't late," I said, setting down my cup and taking both his hands in mine. "Andrew is dead. I'm here. It's all over. It's all over! Maybe if I say it enough, I'll really believe it."

A hint of smile passed over Richard's lips as he gathered me into his arms. Into my ear he said, "It's over, Sarah, and soon we'll put Echo Moon behind us forever!"

Sighing contentedly, I felt the warmth of his broad shoulders beneath my hands and recalled the ease with which he had pulled me to safety.

"Richard, where on earth were you all day, anyway? I kept wanting to talk to you and then kept hoping you'd come with the police. I'd nearly given up hope, you know."

He refilled our cups from the pot on the table nearby as he explained. "We had two shipments to bring over from the mainland, remember? We got the first one here and unloaded, but by then the weather was getting pretty awful. We were halfway across the lake for our second pickup before it really turned ugly, so we had to push on." He grimaced and clutched at his stomach. "I'm a fairweather sailor, and it was a rocky ride! When we got to the shore, we had no choice but to stay put for a while. Hours, as it turned out."

I nodded, then asked, "But how did you know to return with the police? How could you tell I was in trouble?"

Richard shrugged. "It's funny how it happened, actually. We were all sitting around in the storehouse, playing cards and talking. The conversation got around to our employer, Andrew Clayton, and Captain Bill asked if Andrew had any more crates to bring over today."

"Crates?"

"Yes. It seems Andrew frequently had several wooden crates waiting on the dock for the captain to bring to the mainland. The captain didn't know what was in them and said he never asked. The past few weeks, he picked the crates up at night. Got paid extra for it, so he didn't complain. When he told us that, I thought about the lights you saw in the woods. Remember?"

He paused in his story to rub the heels of his hands against his eyes, revealing just how tired he was.

"Well, that got me thinking. What if Andrew and Frank were in this together? I had no idea why, but Andrew's attitude lately seemed to indicate he was capable of anything. In any event, we knew Frank was up to something illegal, and we had Emil's evidence to prove it." He shrugged. "That seemed reason enough to call in the police in a hurry."

"And they believed you — just like that?" I asked.

"I can't say they believed me, actually," Richard said with a grin. "More like interested curiosity on their part, I'd say. But I showed the officer Emil's letter, and they decided there was something to investigate. Maybe they were just planning to humor me. Quite a surprise, then, to find out theft was only one of the crimes being committed."

We fell silent, each of us lost in our own thoughts about the horrors of the day. At last I said, "How is Janet taking all this? She had gone to her room by the time I'd finished talking to the police. I haven't seen her since . . . since it all happened."

Shaking his head, Richard said, "It's been

pretty rough on her, of course. She swears she didn't know anything about the thefts or Frank's involvement in them. I believe her too."

"Oh, yes, so do I. She was as shocked as I was this afternoon. She tried to stop him, you know. But it was no good."

"What I still don't understand is why Andrew continued to systematically spirit away the collections after we were working with them." Richard tipped his cup to drink the last of his coffee. "Did he think we wouldn't notice?"

"Probably. If it weren't for Roland's inventory, I wouldn't have known what should have been in the library and wasn't. I think Andrew was overconfident. He never thought he'd be caught. Frank wouldn't turn him in, he knew that."

"But Frank warned you to stay away," Richard pointed out.

"It's much easier to do that than to admit you were a criminal," I suggested and Richard agreed. "Will Frank go to jail now?" I asked. "What will happen to Janet and the island?"

Richard shrugged. "I'm not a lawyer, so I don't know. The old burglary charge could still stand, but I'd think a judge would go easy on an old man being blackmailed. He's suffered plenty over the years."

"But the island?"

"The island will become a state park and historical site, just as Roland always planned. The Peabodys were to remain on the island as caretakers. Janet told us on your first day here that Roland had provided for their future, remember? I don't think you need to worry too much about them." He patted my hand. "They've made it through over thirty years of uncertainty and worries already. They're survivors."

I swallowed hard before I asked my next question. It was the one that mattered most of all. My cheeks felt hot, and I kept my glance on my hands, clenched together in my lap. "What about us?"

Richard cleared his throat and shifted on the seat next to me. I was holding my breath, anxious for him to speak. An eternity later he did.

"I was thinking you might be interested in opening another bookstore in South Clifton."

My breath came out in a rush as I smiled and teased, "Now, why would I want to do that?"

To my surprise and delight, he covered my hands with his and, looking into my eyes, said softly, "Because a husband and wife should live in the same town. Will you marry me, Sarah?"

Tears sprung to my eyes, and I blinked to clear my vision. My heart felt full to bursting with love and happiness, all my fears and worries gone. "Yes!" I said, squeezing his hands and smiling. "Of course I'll marry you!"

He hugged me then, nearly driving the air from my lungs with the effort. I laughed out loud for what felt like the first time in ages. When Richard's lips met mine, I knew the ghosts of Echo Moon would not haunt our future.

As I rested my cheek against his, my gaze traveled to the huge picture window across the room. Just a sliver of water could be seen through the trees. Calm and still now, the lake glinted silver beneath the glow of a full summer moon.

The employees of Thorndike Press hope you have enjoyed this Large Print book. All our Large Print titles are designed for easy reading, and all our books are made to last. Other Thorndike Press Large Print books are available at your library, through selected bookstores, or directly from us.

For information about titles, please call:

(800) 223-2336

To share your comments, please write:

Publisher
Thorndike Press
P.O. Box 159
Thorndike, Maine 04986